AFTER THE SUMMER PEOPLE LEAVE

AFTER THE SUMMER PEOPLE LEAVE

12 Baffling Adirondack Mystery Stories

by
William T. Lowe

Pinto 🐾 Press
Elizabethtown, NY

The following stories first appeared in the *Alfred Hitchcock Mystery Magazine,* published by Dell Magazines, Inc.: All Indians Are Warriors, So Long, Lana Turner; The Land Healers; A Feeling for the Truth; The Bust of the Year; Your Law, Our Land; Murray and Mister Smart Nose.

Cover illustration and design by Alison Muñoz

Publisher's Cataloging in Publication
(Prepared by Quality Books Inc.)

Lowe, William T., 1920–
    After the summer people leave: 12 baffling
Adirondack mystery stories / by William T. Lowe.
    p. cm.
    LCCN: 96-69805
    ISBN 0-9632476-4-6

    1. Adirondack Mountains Region (N. Y.)—Fiction.
    2. Detective and mystery stories. I. Title.

PS3562.094A48 1996   813'.54
                                       QBI96-40128

First edition: September 1996

To my wife, Joan

Acknowledgments

For their courtesy and assistance my thanks to Trooper Rose Recor, NY State Police; Agent Mark Henry, US Border Patrol; Inspector Karen Kaufman and Chief Inspector Tim Meschinelli, US Customs Service; Ken Jock, Director of the Environmental Division, St. Regis Mohawk Tribe; Kendall Southard, forester; Dennis Aprill, naturalist, and past and present reporters for the Plattsburgh Press-Republican.

Contents

The Smart
Thing to Do

The thing you want to remember about a beaver is that he is smart. Smarter than any other creature on four feet. Smarter than some I know on two feet.

The beaver I call Red Ear had just warned me that somebody was coming through the woods by the pond. I burrowed deeper into a bed of ferns by a maple tree. If this was the man the troopers were looking for he had a gun and he had already wounded one man. I had been told to stay out of sight, not to interfere.

The surface of the pond was smooth and quiet again. Red Ear had slapped his big tail on the water just once and disappeared into his lodge underwater. It was the sound of the slap and the ripples that got my attention. A wildlife expert might say the slap was merely a message to other beavers in the colony and not a warning to me. He might even remind me that beavers are nocturnal, that Red Ear wouldn't be out in the pond in mid-afternoon.

But like I said, a beaver is smart. An animal that can build dams and dig canals and harvest and store food and take time to play with its young doesn't always do what the experts say he should. Red Ear knows I come to the pond every day to have our little game. He and I swap treats. I'll leave him an apple or an ear of corn today and tomorrow I'll find a gift in return, a short piece of young aspen or poplar. He assumes I like to eat what he does.

Off to my left a blue jay began complaining. There are two ways to get here from the county road. One is a path through the swamp, used by fishermen. The other is closer, through the woods and across the beaver dam at the south end of the pond. The blue jay was over there somewhere.

I pushed the Send button on my radio. "Company's coming," I whispered.

"Watch yourself." It was a young trooper named Ben Haley. He was watching the path through the swamp. He is a nice young man, two years out of the academy in Albany, but sometimes he forgets and calls me "pop," which I don't like.

Other state troopers and Border Patrol agents are manning a roadblock out there on the far side of my pond. It's been there since late yesterday when some men tried to hijack a big truck and trailer headed south.

I didn't know about it until last night after dinner. "Masterpiece Theatre" was just going off when there was a knock at the door. It was Newton Call, a trooper I knew before I retired.

"Evenin', Hank. Just came by to tell you what's goin' on. We're tailin' this big tractor-trailer rig coming south from Champlain when somebody tries to take it down. Started shootin' when they wouldn't stop. The driver caught one but he'll be all right. Two men ran into the woods down below your pond; we know one of them is armed. Another guy got away in their car.

"We put up a roadblock just in case. Those two men will come out when they get hungry. They'll probably try to steal some wheels. Nothing for you to worry about, Hank, we'll handle it." At the door Newt turned back. "Best keep your door locked. Just in case."

"Right. Thanks, Newt."

Hijacking is not uncommon around here. In upstate New York we're just over an hour south of the Canadian border. A lot of contraband moves both ways. With narcotics and firearms going north and counterfeit currency and aliens coming south, well, anybody will tell you smuggling is a dog-eat-dog business.

And I did lock my doors.

"We'll handle it, Hank." A polite invitation to stay out of the way. And I would have, except for two reasons. First, I'm a retired deputy sheriff, and second, those men may be hiding on my property.

I came out here to the pond early this morning and found fresh footprints on the path. No way to tell who left them, but I borrowed a little radio from Ben Haley. Like Newt said, just in case.

I heard something move in the brush by the end of the dam. I had my old thirty-eight with me; I took it out of my belt and held it down by my side.

I heard more noises and began to relax. Someone was not very good at being quiet. Then I saw a man step out of the brush into the path, moving very slowly, looking over his shoulder with almost every step.

He was about five-eight, mid-forties, running to fat. He had dark hair and a small mustache. He had been well dressed in town clothes before he spent a night in the woods. His shoes and pants were muddy; there were burdock burrs on his jacket.

I stopped him when he was about ten feet away. I stepped out and showed him my gun. "Raise your hands."

He gasped and almost fell down. "Yes, sir." He stretched both arms up as far as he could. He had a French-Canadian accent.

"Drop your jacket and turn around." He did and I saw he was not armed. He was exhausted; I let him sit down. He looked over his shoulder again, and then at me.

"Please, m'sieur, have you anything to eat? I'm starved. Is this water safe to drink? Is there some place I can call my office?"

I pushed the Send button on the radio again. "You better set another place for dinner," I said.

Five minutes later Ben Haley and another trooper appeared. They gave the little man a drink from a canteen and led him away.

"He give you any trouble?" Haley asked me.

I shook my head. "I knew he was coming."

"How's that?"

"A friend of mine told me."

"His name is Anton Cantillo," a BCI agent named Wade O'Reilly told us. "He's an international arms dealer. Works out of Toronto and Palm Beach. He's never brokered anything major like selling tanks or jet fighters, but he's on everybody's routine surveillance list, the Canadians, the British, Interpol."

The prisoner had been brought to state police headquarters in Ray Brook. The Border Patrol people wanted to take him to their offices in Swanton but they agreed that this was closer.

I tagged along. The little man had been trespassing on my property, and something told me this wasn't a simple case of firearms or liquor smuggling. If you could package curiosity I'd be a rich man.

Now I was seated with Ben Haley and some other people in an office in Troop B's Ray Brook headquarters, a big, modern one-story building, scrupulously clean. The air conditioning was on and it was welcome; September was still sultry.

Wade O'Reilly was a man of about my age. He had taken the trouble to find out who I was; this briefing was as much for my benefit as it was for the others.

"Cantillo will be questioned about what happened yesterday but here's the background," O'Reilly said. "Our Canadian sources alerted us that he was moving some military equipment down into the state. Yesterday he brought a flatbed truck through Customs carrying what his paperwork described as agricultural machinery.

"We followed him because we wanted to arrest him and his contacts on this side. Cantillo had set up a meet at a point on Dry Bridge Road south of Harkness," he nodded at me, "near Mr. Sessions' farm. But somebody else wanted the shipment. Before we could intervene some shooting broke out.

"Cantillo himself fled into the woods and was taken into custody this morning. An unknown man, the gunman, is still at large and on foot. His accomplice disappeared in a late-model car. We have put out a description of it.

"Cantillo's driver, one Felix Mousseau, was wounded and is in the hospital. He is being cooperative. He tells us that Cantillo was carrying twenty-five thousand dollars in cash. It's illegal to bring that much cash into the country with out declaring it, as you know. There's no trace of the money.

"The area of the attempted heist was secured at 1730 hours yesterday and a roadblock detail is on duty. The truck and trailer have been brought here and have been impounded. Any questions?"

Ben Haley held up his hand. "Can you tell us what's on the truck?"

I was curious about that, too. Since the load was big enough to be on a flatbed trailer I thought it might be an armored personnel carrier or a couple of half-tracks. There's a good market for vehicles like that in Mexico.

O'Reilly glanced at me. "I understand that you put in some time in Nam, Mr. Sessions?"

"Right. Military Police."

"Then this might be an old friend. Cantillo got his hands on a Huey."

O'Reilly led the way outside to the impound area. Haley touched my arm. "A who-ee. What's that?"

"Not who-ee. Hue-ee," I told him. "Hue-ee. It's a helicopter."

"Really? Did you use those in Vietnam?"

He wasn't even in high school back then. I hadn't thought about Nam in a long time. "Yes, we did," I said.

A big Peterbilt tractor hitched to a long flatbed trailer was parked inside the high fence. The trailer was loaded with large wooden crates strapped down to the bed. Some had been partially opened; I climbed up and looked inside. It was a Huey, once a proud little aircraft now dissected by some battlefield scavenger and crammed into some ugly wooden crates.

I looked away from the buildings at the Whiteface mountain range to the north. White cumulus clouds hung motionless over the pine and hardwood forests.

I had seen clouds like that in Nam, hanging over jungle so thick that every step was an effort. Sometimes Charlie would be all around, waiting to finish off a squad. A little chopper like this one would appear low over the trees, rotors beating down the tall grass, ignoring fire from the ground, to snatch up the wounded and streak back to the rear.

I went over and stood beside O'Reilly. "What will happen to it?"

"Cantillo had it sold to an aircraft museum down in Texas. They may still get it if he can show a clear title, but I doubt he can. Meantime it's confiscated. We'll turn it over to the National Guard."

Ben Haley chimed in. "We ought to have the Guard put it back together and put it on display in the shopping center up in Plattsburgh," he offered. "A lot of people are still interested in Vietnam, you know."

That rubbed me the wrong way. "Maybe you could take it down to Albany and put it on the lawn in front of the veterans' hospital."

"Sure, pop, we could do that," Ben said, "but a lot more people would see it at the mall."

I drove home thinking about Nam. When we pulled out in 1975 the army walked away and left mountains of materiel behind. Millions of dollars worth, abandoned. Over nine hundred aircraft, including Dragonfly jets and Hueys. Almost a thousand ships and boats. Forty thousand trucks. All kinds of ammunition and over seven hundred thousand M-16 rifles.

All left behind, disowned. The army hurried back to the Pentagon to supervise the production of six-hundred-dollar hammers and twelve-hundred-dollar toilet seats. And of course there was a fire sale of our military hardware in Asia and the Middle East. No doubt Vietnam sold some of the stuff to third-world countries not on our Christmas card list.

Now a small-time arms dealer wanted to sell a Huey chopper to some aircraft collectors in Texas. I hoped they would get it. They could park it on a flight line along with some other obsolete birds like the P-40 and the B-17. Those planes made a difference and I think they deserve a little respect.

When I got home I put an apple in my pocket and headed back to the pond. I wanted to take a look around; that other man might still be in the area. But after all the traffic this morning there were too many footprints to tell me anything. I did see the trail Anton Cantillo had made.

He'd thought he was being followed. Instead of taking the path that skirted the end of the pond he crossed on the top of the beaver dam. That's not an easy walk even for me, but Anton was anxious to avoid a man who wanted to put him in the nearest emergency room. Even so he was lucky to get across even if he did get his shoes and pants all muddy.

I sat down under my maple tree and looked out over the pond. It's small as ponds go, just a little bit over two acres. It has the usual pond life, small fish, frogs, ducks in the autumn. And it's an ideal home for Red Ear and the families in his colony.

One day this spring I brought my lunch out here; it was before black fly season. I happened to throw an apple core into the water. There was a sudden swirl and a sleek black head appeared and grabbed the core before it sank. That was Red Ear. He's a young adult, maybe four years old, and thirty pounds or so in weight. He has intelligent eyes and tiny flat ears. There is a faint red spot on the left one which is why I call him Red Ear.

8

It took a long time to work out our little game. There's a flat rock by the water's edge and that's where I leave his treat, an apple cut into quarters. He can swim right up to get it, no need to come ashore. And that's where I find my gift, a short piece of a small limb, aspen or birch. Sometimes I also get something else like an empty soda can. Once it was a hat lost by a fisherman.

I save my collection of sticks and when frost comes I put them in the pond near the dam to add to the beavers' winter food supply. They don't hibernate; they stay active even when I don't.

Red Ear is very inquisitive; I know he watches me. I've seen his little black head making a vee in the water near the bank. I think he would avoid a trap, but I try to make sure there aren't any around the pond. Any trap I find is cut apart and hung in a tree as a notice to its owner.

A red-tailed hawk glided silently over the trees and out of sight. It was one of those absolutely still moments that come with the end of a day here in the mountains. The pond was blue glass. The sun had left brilliant streaks of color. Then a breeze hurried across the surface of the water and the ripples were all the colors of the sky. Miss Emily Dickinson once said the wind was like a busy housewife wielding a broom. I had just seen her come back to dust the pond.

When the colors faded I put Red Ear's apple on the flat rock and went home.

After dinner I began wondering again about that second man. I phoned Ray Brook and found that Ben Haley was off duty. I got a number for Wade O'Reilly, probably his car phone. He told me they thought the man had stolen a car and was headed south.

Anton Cantillo was in no hurry to go back to Canada. "Doesn't want to go back and face the music for losing the shipment. Says the hijacker got the twenty-five thou'."

Wade said they would disband the roadblock in the morning.

The morning mist was lifting from the pond when I got there. It would be another perfect day in the Adirondacks. In a month the hardwood trees would be in color. I walked to the water's edge and couldn't believe my eyes when I looked at the flat stone.

Of course the apple was gone but in its place was something strange. It was a green leather pouch, about ten inches long, the kind cashiers use when they go to the bank. It had been in the water; it was wet.

I picked up the pouch and opened the zipper and looked inside. It was filled with one hundred and five hundred dollar bills. I took some of the bills out; a few were damp, the rest were dry. I stood there like a statue, thinking.

Yes, the pouch was a gift from Red Ear to me, a substitute for the usual short piece of young aspen or birch. But where had the beaver found it? And could this be the money the arms dealer Anton Cantillo was carrying, the twenty-five thousand his driver told O'Reilly about? It had been just yesterday that Cantillo stood right here, cold and hungry.

From behind me a man's voice said, "I'll take that money."

I turned around to see a man standing behind me with a gun pointed at my chest. He had a heavy, jowly face and wore dirty street clothes. I didn't like the look on his face, he seemed desperate and that could make him dangerous.

"So you got the little guy's dough. Put it on the ground, old man."

His gun was one of the new automatics. My pistol was on the top shelf at home where I had left it. I stooped and put the money and the pouch on the ground.

"I think it's counterfeit," I said. That just might confuse him. It didn't.

"Shut up, old man."

To be behind me he must have followed me here. Maybe he had been hiding in the orchard by my house. He had to be the man who had followed Cantillo into the woods and been deserted by his partner.

"I want the keys to that pickup by the house," he said, moving the gun upwards to point at my face.

"Sorry," I said. "The keys are in the truck."

"You're lying. I looked. Turn out your pockets."

Should I try to stall him? I noticed that now the woods were quiet, very quiet. Then from out in the pond I heard a slap on the water, a slap made by a beaver's tail.

It couldn't be a coincidence, I told myself. Beavers have superb hearing. Red Ear had heard somebody coming yesterday. Maybe he had again just now. It might cost me to find out, maybe a bullet, but I would stall, play for time.

I looked over the man's shoulder. "Hey, fellows," I said in what I hoped was a cheerful, buddy-buddy voice, "look at what crawled out from under a rock."

I raised my hand and waved vigorously at the empty path behind him.

The man smirked at the old trick. It was feeble and childish but it was all I could think of.

"That won't work, old man. Shut up or I'll crack your skull."

I took a step backwards; I tried to laugh a little, still looking past him. "Look at this piece of garbage, guys."

I waved again and pointed at the man. Another step backward.

The man frowned but he kept his eyes on my face. "Hey, I got it!" I said in my idiot's voice. "Somebody left the cage open and the monkey got out!"

The cheap insults finally made the man furious. "I told you, old man!" He drew back his hand to aim a blow at my head. "Now you're going to get it!"

I was at the water's edge; there was nowhere I could go. But that wasn't a problem. Five seconds ago I had seen Ben Haley come around the bend in the path with his gun drawn. Now he was behind the stranger.

"Not today, buster." Ben jammed his gun into the man's spine. "Drop the piece."

The man began cursing but he dropped his gun. I ignored him and leaned against a birch tree and took some deep breaths. Ben and another trooper took over. Afterwards Ben gave me a worried look.

"What were you trying to do, pop, needling him like that? You could have got yourself killed."

"I knew you were back there in the woods."

He was incredulous. "I suppose a friend told you."

"In fact, yes." I was all out of cute banter. "You just drop in for coffee?"

"Nope. We're pulling out the roadblock. Just taking a last look around." He picked up the money and the pouch.

"I see you found Cantillo's bankroll. How'd you know where to look for it?"

I shrugged. "Long story."

Ben stuffed the bills back into the pouch and zipped it shut. "Cantillo sent for me last night. Said he wanted to make a deal. Told me he had hidden his dough out here and he would split it with you and me if we retrieved it for him. Told me about what he thought was a beaver dam and a big pile of sticks. Trusting soul, isn't he?"

That was the end of it. "Another day, another prisoner," Ben said as they left. "Let's don't make a habit of this, Mr. Sessions."

"I won't if you won't. Say hi to O'Reilly for me."

I really wasn't surprised that Red Ear had found that money pouch. Beavers have an instinct that says 'no littering allowed'. They keep their lodges and underwater surroundings clear of foreign objects, hats, gloves, tin cans, landing nets. Even a green leather pouch.

Why did Red Ear bring the money pouch to me? Because it was the smart thing to do. Along with his apple that day he got a bonus of two carrots and an ear of corn.

All Indians
Are Warriors

T he van had no business in Rory's barn, especially
a van loaded with illegal slot machines. And especially this close to the St. Regis Indian Reservation,
where slot machines had caused something of a civil
war.

Rory had come home and found Major, his son's
pony, grazing on what was left of the summer's flowerbeds. He led Major back to the barn, and there parked
inside the big double doors was the van. He opened the
rear doors and looked inside. In the cargo section were
ten slot machines. No names, no addresses. Rory stood
and frowned at the contraband cargo.

Like most Mohawks, his hair was jet black and die
straight. He wore it shoulder length, caught with a bit
of ribbon. He had the typical Indian's heavy chin and
strong nose; his eyes were a surprisingly light brown.

Had somebody made a mistake? Not likely—ten
slots represented too much money for casual error. It
had to be a frame; someone wanted him in trouble. But
who? The Warrior Society, perhaps. They had resented

his pacifist stand in the gambling wars just a few weeks ago.

The van didn't tell him anything. It was a light delivery model, no registration, no ignition key, New York plates. The hood was slightly warm. This was a brisk October day; Rory judged the van couldn't have been here longer than two hours. Somebody knew his schedule.

"Your name Rory Horn?"

Rory whirled around; in the open barn door stood two troopers. They were in the full uniform of the New York state police, with the new Glock 17 automatic at the belt. They were both white.

"I'm Rory Horn." So it was a frame. Plant the slots in Rory's barn, call the troopers, watch Rory go to jail. But somehow that didn't seem like the Warriors' style.

The taller trooper lounged against the door frame. "You going to start up your own casino, Rory?" he said easily. "I'll come deal twenty-one for you."

Rory shook his head. "Not me. I never saw that van or those slots before right now."

"No, of course not," the second trooper said sarcastically. He hooked his thumbs in his belt. "Come on, you're going with us." His tone and posture were meant to be intimidating.

Rory knew this type of white man. They could work around Indians, but they never learned to trust them, were even a bit afraid of them. To this white man Rory and his kind were smart-ass Indians. To the Indians they were clay-headed white men.

"Hold on," Rory said to the first trooper. "What brought you fellows up here? You got a search warrant?"

"Now, Rory," the trooper said gently, "this door here is standing wide open. We're not searching, we're just standing here looking in. We just happened to observe those slot machines."

"Right," said the second trooper belligerently. "This is simple observation. And we got a call from a friend of yours."

"A friend who said I had some stolen property?"

"That's right."

"He didn't give his name, of course."

"That's right. Let's go."

"Just a minute," Rory snapped. He turned and walked to the other side of the barn. He forked hay into Major's stall, added grain, checked the water bucket. Then he walked back to the doorway. "I'll leave a note for my wife," he said.

"No time for that," the second trooper said. "Let's go." Rory whirled on him, "Am I under arrest?"

"Well, no."

"Then I'm leaving a note."

On the way to Massena in the police car Rory thought about the recent conflict on the reservation. The issue was gambling; slot machines were the biggest and most irritating part of the problem.

The Akwesasne Mohawks were divided on the issue of casino gambling. One faction wanted open casinos, Las Vegas style. The other wanted no part of that; bingo was enough. Confrontation between the two had been heated, at times violent. A predawn shootout had left two men dead.

The state police had come in to try to maintain peace. They had confiscated the slot machines in the casinos; slots are illegal in New York. There had been strenuous opposition. The militant Warriors Society viewed the police as intruders in a sovereign nation. There had been gunfire and barricades and casualties.

The New York newspapers called it the "gambling wars."

Today the big casinos were shuttered and dark. The highways were open again, but it was an uneasy truce. Tensions were high and all sides alert for trouble. And now ten illegal slot machines had appeared in Rory's barn, ready to bring grief to anyone who came near them.

At the police substation in Massena Rory stood in front of a desk while a sergeant filled out a form.

"Your name?" he asked in a bored voice.

"O-Karatsisto."

The sergeant looked up. "No, I want your English name."

"Rorhare Horn."

"I thank you."

The lieutenant seemed to know all about the van in Rory's barn. He also seemed to know that Rory was a valued employee of the Seaway Authority and had no record of any kind. He would have been happy for Rory to admit that he was babysitting the slot machines for an unnamed third party for an undisclosed sum of money, but Rory did not oblige him. He repeated that he knew nothing of the ownership of the van or its cargo.

The interview was short. Rory felt the lieutenant was just going through the motions of questioning him. He even thanked Rory for coming in. Rory was relieved; if the frame was supposed to result in his arrest it had somehow misfired.

In the hall a familiar voice stopped him. Rory turned and saw an old friend, a young white man in a trooper's uniform. Rory and Nash Seymour had gone to high school together in Salmon River. After that they had grown apart, Rory to go to college and Nash into law enforcement.

"What'd you do, Rory? Steal somebody's horse?"

"If I had, it would take more than you guys to catch me."

They shook hands warmly. "What's going on, Rory?"

Nash became serious when Rory told him about the slot machines. "I hope we don't start that all over again," Nash said. He had been on the roadblocks during the siege with the Mohawks.

"I hope not, too."

"Say, how are you going to get home? You still live out near Helena?" Nash reached into his pocket. "Take my car. My shift's just started; I won't need it until tomorrow."

"Thanks, Nash, I appreciate it."

"Watch yourself, Rory."

"You, too, Nash. Remember the old saying: be nice to your enemies; it bugs the hell out of them."

Nash grinned. "What big Mohawk chief said that?"

Rory shook his head. "It was a paleface. Fellow name of Oscar Wilde."

As Rory passed the front desk the sergeant stood up and stopped him.

"If you don't mind, son, what does your Indian name mean?"

Rory smiled. "It means Child of the Evening Star,"

The sergeant nodded. "Real nice."

Rory drove through the reservation on his way home. At the western boundary he passed a small souvenir shop. A sign on the roof read:

—WELCOME TO AKWESASNE—
LAND WHERE THE PARTRIDGE DRUMS

The shop was closed, and weeds grew in its driveway. Few visitors ventured onto the reservation these days. The constant presence of the state police was not inviting, and now winter was coming.

Route 37 widened into Hogansburg's Main Street. On either side were the closed and dark casinos, their vast parking lots empty. There were frequent rumors that the governor and the gaming commission would permit the casinos to reopen, but the days became weeks and the casinos stood empty and silent, their employees idle and restless.

Rory passed the American Legion post on his left; on his right was the ornate Church of Christ, its massive stone walls stretching for almost a full block. Rory watched his rear-view mirror; a vehicle had pulled out of the Bear's Den service station and was following him.

It was probably a Warrior patrol, one of many that roamed the reservation. Rory decided to pull over; he was driving a strange car. He stopped and stepped out.

A jeep parked behind him. In it sat two men dressed in army camouflage gear and wearing combat boots. One held an AK 47 assault rifle in his arms; the other carried a shotgun. The Warriors were organized and well armed. And they were very contentious. "If you are not with us, you are against us."

Rory knew the man with the automatic weapon; it was Jake Hightower, one of the Warrior leaders. He lifted a hand in greeting.

Jake stepped out of the jeep, leaving his weapon behind. He was much taller than Rory; he bent his head to speak. "The troopers giving you a hard time, Rory?"

Rory knew that the story of the van and the slot machines and his visit to Massena would cover the reservation by nightfall.

"Trying to," he admitted.

"You want me to have a team watch your house for awhile? Guard any valuable property you might have out there?"

This offer of protection would be a big favor, but a favor that would have to be repaid some day. "Thanks, Jake, but I think I can handle it."

"Suit yourself." The big Warrior stepped back and returned to his jeep. Rory headed out on 37. It was dark, and he was anxious to get home.

Like many Mohawks Rory lived off the reservation. Housing was scarce there, and his home in Helena was close to Donna's job at the Tru-Stitch factory in Bombay. Their home was a neat, compact trailer that had been fitted with a weather-tight entrance in front and a large deck in back.

The house and land were his legacy. Rory's father had belonged to a special group of Mohawks, the high-steel workers. He and the others worked on the skyscrapers in New York City. Each Monday, well before dawn, they traveled down to raise the skyline of Manhattan still higher. On Friday nights they came back to their families, bearing big paychecks just as their forefathers had returned from the hunt bearing game. His father had insisted Rory go to college, to learn to depend on his mind instead of ice-cold nerves and bowstring reflexes.

Several oak trees shaded his driveway; tonight their heavy shadows concealed three men. After Rory parked and stepped out of his car, they advanced noiselessly. Rory was surprised to see that one of the men was Chief Douglas Solomon. This had to be a very important mission to bring one of the tribal council chiefs in person.

Chief Solomon was a dignified, middle-aged Mohawk. Behind him stood two Warriors. One carried a Rugers .223 rifle, the other a twelve-gauge shotgun. Rory knew these were the prescribed Warrior weapons.

"Evening, Mr. Horn," Chief Solomon said, as casually as if they had met on a street in Hogansburg.

"Chief," Rory said politely. He glanced again at the weapons and thought of Donna and Rory Junior in the house.

"Forgive the intrusion," Chief Solomon said. "We happen to be most interested in that van parked in your barn. With your permission these men will keep it under observation tonight. Just out of curiosity, you understand."

"I understand." One of the troopers from this afternoon had been detailed to guard the van until it could be towed away. If he had a choice, he would prefer to have these Warriors on guard duty tonight.

"Two things, Chief Solomon," Rory said respectfully. The chief inclined his head graciously.

"I hope it will not become necessary to disturb my family," Rory said.

The chief nodded. "It is to be avoided."

Rory went on. "The state police may also be watching," he said. He could not resist adding, "What is in the van is not my property."

"We understand, Mr. Horn. Have a pleasant evening." The three Indians faded into the shadows. The night was silent. Rory looked up at the sky. Stars were beginning to appear as he went inside the house.

Dinner was late, and afterward Rory sat by his son's bed and told him stories about smart foxes and big bears and giant moose and stalwart Indians. Rory Junior drifted off to sleep, clutching his favorite toy, a stuffed giraffe.

Rory and Donna sat at the kitchen table and talked in low voices. "Did you call Uncle Mark?" Rory asked. He had put this request in the note he had left that afternoon.

"I called and left a message at the Red Arrow Gift Shop. That's the procedure, isn't it?"

"Right." Mark Benjamin had been a friend of Rory's father. Very few people knew that "Uncle Mark" was a senior agent in the New York State Bureau of Criminal Investigation.

"You think Uncle Mark can find out who planted those machines in our barn?" Donna's expression was serious, but she was not frightened. She was a non-native, a white girl Rory had met when they were both college students at Potsdam. They had dated for a year and had been married after graduation.

"I hope so."

Donna poured more coffee. "What's so wrong with slot machines anyway?" she said. "Bingo, lotteries, OTB, slots, what's the difference?"

Rory frowned at his cup. "First of all, there are different forms of gambling," he said slowly. "Ritualistic gambling is a strong part of the Mohawk tradition. The federal government accepts the fact that almost all Indian nations have spiritual games of chance. They might not understand it, but they accept it.

"The Federal Indian Gaming Act permits bingo and some card games on Indian reservations. The people here who want casinos also want slot ma chines because there's big money to be made with slot machines. And that's the problem. In the state of New York, slot machines are illegal. Period."

Donna nodded. "And some of the tribe feel we are a sovereign nation and not subject to New York law."

Rory held up his hand and Donna fell silent. He was listening intently. The usual night sounds were gone. He thought he heard a faint sound from the direction of the barn. Donna was watching him. "What is it?" she whispered.

Then the night was torn by the rapid pounding of a heavy gun, frighteningly loud. Without conscious thought Rory grabbed Donna's hand and pulled her with him to the floor.

There was a second burst of fire, louder and closer. The light switch was on the wall above his head; Rory lunged upward and struck the switch with the side of his hand, plunging the kitchen into darkness.

He lay still, trying not to breathe. From the highway came the sound of a car receding into the night. There was a whimper from the next room where Rory Junior lay sleeping. Then nothing, no sound at all.

"Stay down," he whispered to Donna. He rolled to the door, stretched up for the knob, threw himself through the opening into the darkness. He thought he caught the smell of burnt cordite in the air. In the starshine, shadows gradually took shape; two of them moved toward him. Two men.

"Just a couple of prowlers," one of the Warriors said. "They won't be back." He moved away into the night.

"Hi, kid," said Mark Benjamin, his hand outstretched. "Sorry I'm late for the party."

Mark Benjamin could have been any age from forty-five to sixty. He had a deeply tanned and lined face and innocent blue eyes that somehow inspired confidence. He always dressed in an old-fashioned corduroy suit with a chain across the vest. The suit also seemed to inspire confidence. Benjamin was stationed in Syracuse, but he spent most of his time in the field as an almost independent BCI agent.

Seated at the kitchen table, Mark looked like a successful insurance salesman. "Nothing like a hot cup of good coffee on a cold night," he said with a grateful smile at Donna. Then to Rory he said, "And nothing like a few slot machines to stir things up, eh, Rory?"

"You're right there. What's so special about those machines somebody dumped on me?"

"Those are very special," Mark said with a broad grin, "because nobody knows where they came from, and nobody knows who's controlling them."

He hitched his chair closer and lowered his voice. "You both remember when the state police confiscated the slots in the Nevada World and the other casinos. There was a hell of a dust-up, and the casinos got closed down. Now our office hears that some of the chiefs are close to an agreement with the gaming commission to reopen the casinos. I don't know the details; maybe there'll be some form of supervision, some kind of tax, whatever. But when the green light comes, the Nevada World and the other houses will want slots, and fast, right?"

Donna and Rory nodded. Mark continued. "Now, there's a crime family that wants this slot business. They want to get their feet in the door with slots and go on from there—bring in their own dealers, have their own security, get a bigger and bigger cut of the take. This family is headed by a gent named Dominic Farillo, called Dommy behind his back. And our Dommy thinks he has been a very smart boy. He's got ninety or a hundred slots up here right now, hidden in old barns and empty shacks around little towns like Brasher and Helena, all ready to deliver to the casinos."

"Who gets there first gets the business, right?" asked Donna, her eyes shining.

"And those ten slots on our doorstep are part of his stock?" asked Rory.

"Right, Donna. Wrong, Rory," said Mark, grinning. "That's the beauty part. Those ten slots are wild cards. They're not Dommy's. Now, Dommy has to think two things. First, he's got competition for the Mohawk casino business, and that steams him. Second, he thinks somebody may have hijacked some of his machines, and that steams him even worse.

"So now Dommy will make a mistake," Mark said gleefully. "He's got to come up here and check on his inventory, see if any slots are missing. When we catch him on the ground with his slots, we'll put him away. Trafficking in illegal gaming devices."

"So the ten slots are bait to sucker Dommy." Donna clapped her hands. "That's cool, Uncle Mark!"

Rory agreed. "But why are the chiefs so uptight?"

"Like I said, Solomon and some others are trying to work out a basis for reopening with the commission. They don't want a bunch of slot machines turning up at the casinos like a shipment of paper towels. It would show bad faith, queer the whole deal. Solomon wants to see those slots safely locked up in the police impound yard, and no place else. You copy?"

In his enthusiasm Mark failed to note the growing look of consternation on Donna's face, the comprehension dawning in Rory's eyes.

"Now, there's another angle," Mark went on. "A couple of people might suspect there's a new player in the game. Someone with slots to sell or lease or whatever. Someone who is advertising for new business. They might want to talk a deal with this mystery man, and they'll figure you, kid, for his local agent."

"Me?"

"You, son. It's your barn, isn't it?"

"Wait a minute, Uncle Mark," said Donna. "Did you ..."

"Wait a minute, Uncle Mark," said Rory. "You did! You brought in that van, you called the police, you squared that lieutenant, you tipped off the chief, *you set up the whole thing!*"

Mark nodded happily. "Pretty neat, eh? I knew you'd like it." He looked from Donna to Rory, and his smile faded. "You do like it, don't you? Now don't get mad, Rory. "

Next morning Rory sat at his desk in Hogansburg and tried to study some field reports. His office was in the new Mohawk Council Administration Building on Memorial Street, a severely modern structure that would have been a credit to IBM or DuPont. But Rory was oblivious to the bright colors and sleek furniture around him. He was thinking of the trap in which he had unknowingly been part of the bait.

"I hope it works," he had told Uncle Mark, "but leave me out of it from here on in."

Rory worked for the St. Lawrence Seaway Authority. He had begun on the lofty International Bridge that spanned the river and connected Canada and the United States. In college he had specialized in environmental science. This year he was on a leave of absence from the Authority to work on the pollution project. For decades the St. Lawrence, which flowed through the res ervation, had been polluted by industrial plants upstream. Now a massive cleanup oper ation was underway, and it was Rory's job to see that the Indians' traditional hunting, fishing, and land rights were respected.

His phone rang. "Dommy's moving," Uncle Mark said. "Private plane to the Clinton County airport. Headed for Fort Covington in a rental. We're on him."

"Good. Let me know when it's over."

"Right, kid."

Five minutes later the phone rang again. "Could we meet at the Nevada this morning, Mr. Horn? We have much to talk about." It was Chief Solomon.

He couldn't concentrate on the field reports anyway. "I'll be there in fifteen minutes," Rory said.

They met in a private room on the top floor. An armed Warrior admitted him at a side door. On his way to the stairs, Rory glanced at the rows of gaming tables shrouded in dustcovers, the stocked bars, the huge wagon wheel chandeliers, the vacant wall spaces where slot machines had been ranked.

The room was quite large. A window facing west looked toward the mammoth Eisenhower Locks through which moved ocean commerce bound for the Great Lakes. In a glass case against a wall was a stunning example of Akwesasne basket weaving: a graceful, intricate work of sweet grass and thin strips of black ash. Rory recognized it from pictures he had seen as a duplicate of the gift presented to Pope John Paul II by the Mohawk nation.

Rory sat facing Solomon across a table. "I think I know your position, Mr. Horn," said Solomon in a condescending tone. "You don't object to gambling, but you do object to violence."

"Right."

"You would like to see the money generated by casinos kept in the community to do good works, correct?"

He was being talked to like a schoolchild, and Rory resented it. He felt his cheeks begin to redden, but he answered the question.

"Yes, I would. Who wouldn't? The old folks home needs repair, the ambulance units need new equipment, the town needs a police force... "

Solomon held up his hand. "I know all that. What makes you think I don't want those things, too? I live here the same as you do. But, Mr. Horn, everything is not always black and white."

There was the patronizing tone Rory resented. He pulled his feet together under his chair.

"All right, Chief Solomon, let me ask you something." He jumped to his feet and leaned across the table. "The big hang-up here is slot machines. They're illegal in New York. They're dirty with mob money."

Rory swung his arm to indicate the room and the building. "Why the hell can't you have a good casino without slots? You can have everything else, wheels, poker, bingo. I hear that's enough for other reservation casinos. Where do you get off being so stubborn about the goddamn slots?"

Rory shut up and sat down. I went too far, he told himself. He tried to frame an apology; then he was aware that Chief Solomon was laughing gently.

"It will surprise you to know that I'm way ahead of you on that, Rory." Rory stared at him, and Solomon smiled. "All I want is a clean operation. If it's without slots, great."

The chief leaned across the table. "Besides, they've got electronic gaming devices now that make those things in your barn look like antique junk. Things that would draw crowds from all over the East Coast. But, Rory, we've got a long way to go."

The chief was quite serious now. "The police invaded our land and took our property. Some of the men want reparation for that, and you can't blame them. If we get the casinos open again, we may have federal supervision, inspectors telling us what to do. Some of the men won't stand for that. Sure, some of us may be too bullheaded, and some of us may be too proud, but we've got to... "

The door opened suddenly, and a man stepped inside. He put his back to the door and locked it. He wore a business suit with a white shirt and silk tie. And a short-barreled .38 revolver which was pointed at Rory. The man was panting as if he had run up the stairs, but the gun was quite steady.

"Dominic Farillo," Solomon murmured to Rory. He took a step forward. "Mr. Farillo," he said, "do you have an appointment?"

Farillo gestured him back with the gun. "Keep out of this, chief." His eyes were on Rory. "You must be Horn, Rory Horn, right?"

Rory nodded. He raised his hands level with his chest.

"You bastard! You set me up. The Feds are all over me." He took a step toward Rory. "Why didn't you come to me first? We could have cooked a deal. Having an Indian like you on the inside would have kept things real smooth."

Rory glanced around him. There was no weapon in sight, not even a paperweight on the table. Solomon stood several feet away. There was nothing, and the gun was pointed right at his chest.

Farillo's face was white with rage. Moisture ran from one side of his mouth. "I gave the Feds the slip, but I gotta keep movin'. You cost me a bundle, Indian, and I'm gonna blast you for it." He drew back the hammer of the gun. Suddenly Rory thought of a story he had told Rory Junior—what the Indian had done when he met the bear in the woods.

Rory threw back his head and stretched his mouth wide. A loud, strident war cry rang out in the room, rising in pitch, bouncing from the walls, an unearthly paean of defiance.

Dommy stood transfixed, petrified, his eyes wide in fear. From the floor Rory swung an uppercut that had one hundred and seventy pounds of angry Indian behind it. His fist caught Dommy on the side of the jaw. Dommy reeled back ward two steps and collapsed.

"Damn!" Solomon gasped. "Damn!" He stepped over and kicked the gun into a corner. "For somebody who doesn't want to be a Warrior, you certainly give a hell of an imitation. You even scared me!"

Rory massaged his hand. He wouldn't admit how sore it was. "I tell my son the stories my father told me."

Solomon nodded. "I remember. You know, all Indians are Warriors when the pressure is on."

They became aware of a pounding on the door. Solomon stepped over and opened it. Two Warriors rushed in, weapons ready. Solomon motioned to the man on the floor. In a minute he had been bound and gagged. The Indians looked at Rory respectfully as they carried the limp form away.

"That piece of dirt will be placed where Mr. Mark Benjamin and his people will find him," said the chief, "and within the hour."

Solomon smiled at the expression on Rory's face. "Oh, yes, we know who our friends are. The list includes a large number of white men."

Rory wasn't listening; he was tired. Maybe he would go home early today, help Rory Junior saddle up Major to do some riding. Then have a quiet evening with his son and Donna. And keep the phone off the hook. The chief was still talking in his confident tone of voice. "We will solve this problem, Rory, with the help of people like yourself. Remember, we've got an edge over the white man."

He looked at Rory expectantly. "Oh, right," Rory said, "we were here first."

He crossed to the door and opened it. "So long, chief. I'm taking the rest of the day off."

A New Way
Every Day

I had forgotten how noisy it can be inside a helicopter. I was riding in the cargo area with a National Guard tech sergeant and a New York state trooper. They were in uniform; I was a guest, on the log book as a civilian consultant.

I pointed at a patch of green on the ground. At two thousand feet it looked like a postage stamp. In the strong autumn sunshine it was emerald green, almost neon bright. I touched the tech's arm.

"Marijuana," I said.

He glanced at a map taped to a big piece of plywood. There were several red circles on the map. "We've got that one," he said.

Below us was a section of the Adirondack Mountains in Essex County, New York. The Guard makes flights like this to search for marijuana, little cultivated patches in open fields or along streams. I had asked to come along to check out a hunch of mine. I'm a retired deputy sheriff; I used to hunt pot growers in these hills years ago, and I think I still have a feeling for it.

In my day the use of pot was mostly recreational. Now it's a business, and growing bigger every year. In the three counties of northern New York it's a cash crop, like apples and corn and hay.

Law enforcement agencies haven't been asleep. In 1989 the National Guard formed a Counterdrug Detachment to work with the state police and local authorities. That's how I happened to be riding in a Guard chopper loaded with surveillance gear.

The game plan was to locate stands of marijuana plants, from the air and on foot, and keep them under observation. When the grower came around to inspect his crop he would be nabbed. If he managed to evade arrest the state police would confiscate the plants at harvest time and destroy them.

I had told the pilot, a Guard lieutenant, the area I wanted to cover. The little town of Jay appeared and I spotted the covered bridge over the Ausable River. The pilot banked to follow Route 9. Through my glasses I was watching for the Blumbard farm. It is about two miles down river from where the John Fountain Road joins Route 9 and a little south of the big granite quarry. It sits across the highway from the river.

"There it is," I said on the intercom as the farm slid behind us.

The pilot made a leisurely turn and came back. He slowed our speed until we were almost hovering. My stomach went up three points on the queasy scale.

The tech bent over a control panel and twisted some dials. Mounted in the nose of the chopper was a heat-sensing device. The thing was incredibly sensitive; if you struck a match anywhere a hundred yards away it would instantly pinpoint your position.

A needle jumped on a scale and the tech turned around and grinned at me. "Bingo," he said. "You're right, Mr. Sessions, that barn is hot."

The state trooper marked our location on a big photo blowup. "Looks like we're going visiting," he said. I was pretty sure I would be invited to go along.

Three days before my helicopter ride I was sitting on my front porch about to take a nap when Leon came to see me. He's a young trooper. He graduated from the Academy in Albany last year and is assigned to Troop B over in Ray Brook. He's tall and thin and still looks eighteen. That's why he draws a lot of undercover assignments.

Instead of making small talk he handed me a leaflet.

GROW YOUR OWN!
ELIMINATE THE MIDDLEMAN!
BE THE ENVY OF YOUR FRIENDS!

If you think Mexican Gold is great wait 'til you try Panama Pride! It's easy to grow your own. Start your own seeds in a coffee can, then plant them in a sunny spot and step back. Will grow to five feet or more in one short season with a little water and TLC. All for you—and your friends. Drop your name and address and a five dollar bill in the old 88. Fast, confidential service!

"Damn," I said. "Where'd this come from?"

"They're all over the school," Leon told me. He meant the big central school outside Clintonville. The leaflet was poorly printed, about six-by-nine, on cheap stock. Of course it was talking about marijuana. Maybe there was a strain called Panama Pride, maybe not. The leaflet would be the topic of conversation all over school.

"I guess you know pot use has gone way up," Leon said.

"I know! I read the papers!" Marijuana use is up twenty per cent nationally, that much and more here. More young lives wasted, sometimes snuffed out.

"Didn't mean to snap at you, Leon. Here, have some lemonade."

"Thanks, Uncle Hank."

Leon calls me Uncle Hank but he's not really a relative. His father and I did a hitch in the military police some wars back.

I looked at the leaflet again. "This has got to be a scam. Get the money and run."

He nodded. "That's what Captain Morris thinks. But we've got to check it out."

"Of course," I said. Even if it was a rip-off it would do a lot of harm by just attracting attention. More kids would experiment, take that first step downward.

Leon cleared his throat. "We're wondering if you would have the time to do some checking, Uncle Hank. You know, anybody with new money."

"Sure, Leon, I'll be glad to."

I held up the leaflet. "This could be Post Office Box 88 in Jay. Or Fountain. Or it could be be a locker at school. Maybe someone's wearing 88 on his uniform."

"Right." He stood up to leave.

"One other thing, Leon," I said. "Pushers aren't going to like any potential competition one little bit. Have some copies of this thing made and spread them around in the right places in Keeseville and Plattsburgh. Might get you some anonymous tips."

"Good idea. We'll do that." He shook his head. "Joe Camel was bad enough. What's next, Peter Pot?"

"Maybe Gertrude Grass. No law says women can't be pushers."

"Why not? Well, see you, Uncle Hank."

"Say hello to your folks."

Grow your own. Cannabis, to use its formal name, is fairly easy to grow if you know what you are doing. Somebody could make some money with this scheme. Maybe he was planning to sell the tiny little seeds. Maybe he had an angle I hadn't thought of.

Years ago when I was a young deputy, pot growers would plant their marijuana in the middle of a corn field where it wouldn't be seen. Frequently we got an anonymous tip and arrested them for possession. Then they sneaked over and planted the stuff in a neighbor's field. Naturally this resulted in many hard feelings.

They got smart and planted on state-owned land of which there are several million acres around here. Then they began stealing each other's plants. That led to security measures like booby traps and armed guards. We lost a few deer and some people did get shot.

A rudimentary science evolved. Pot growers learned that a little cultivation gives a better yield. That there are male and female plants, that pollination takes place as in fruit trees.

A new strain was developed, better suited to our northern climate. A seedless plant was produced with a higher level of THC, which is the psychoactive element in pot.

The local dealers know about the national movement to legalize marijuana and most of them are in favor of it. But obviously a "grow your own" wave would not be in their best interests. Was there a new player in the game?

I like to avoid the heat of the day but now a nap was out of the question. I decided to check out the post office in Fountain. An old schoolmate of mine ran it.

Hannah McCain started out as a window clerk when the post office was in a corner of the general store. She sold stamps and plug tobacco and yard goods. She is as gray as I am now, and there's always a grim look on her face. Either her dentures don't fit right or her feet hurt. Everybody gets the rough side of her tongue.

"Hannah, I have to ask you who rents box 88." We sat at her desk behind the parcel post rack.

"You know I can't tell you that, Hank."

"It's important. Somebody may be selling dope through the mail."

"The hell you say." She glared at me. I showed her the leaflet.

"Damn! What'll the bastards do next? Give out free samples?"

She looked at me and then opened a drawer in her desk and took out a ledger book. "I'm going to the little girls' room," she said, and walked away.

Box 88 was rented to a Reverend Samuel Innes Newburgh. I knew him. The good Baptists of his congregation thought it was funny to call him Brother Sin.

While I had the chance I glanced at Hannah's list. Box 97 was rented to a Jiggs Blumbard with an address on Route 9. The name Blumbard rang a bell. Something about money. Recent money.

When Hannah came back the book was right where she had left it. "By the way, Hannah," I asked, being very casual, "do you know a party named Jiggs Blumbard?"

She snorted. "Your tax dollars at work. Jerk's been on welfare for years."

"He's on one of your rural delivery routes. Why do you suppose he gets the mail here in town?"

"Gives him an excuse to get out of work on his farm. Come to town to get the mail. Hang out at the diner."

"Right." I stood up. "Thanks, Hannah."

"Be careful, Hank." Her tone softened a bit. "What are you going to do now?"

"Get a haircut. Nice seeing you again, Hannah."

A barber shop has always been a good place to ask questions. I sat through a discussion of a new convenience store that might open in town. If it did it would hurt business at Tim Meyer's Sunoco station. Finally I got a chance to mention Jiggs Blumbard's name. I was surprised at the reaction that got. Blumbard was a local celebrity.

Blumbard had a son in junior high school and this spring he had coached the boy to spit on the floor in class. Every class, every day. The school fussed and fumed to no avail. Finally the school board judged the boy to be emotionally disturbed and sent him home. In addition to welfare and disability, Blumbard was now collecting an extra four hundred dollars a month in supplemental income to finance the boy's eventual rehabilitation.

I know the incorrigible child scheme has been used successfully in cities downstate but here in the north country Blumbard was a pioneer. It made him a hero to his cronies. To celebrate Blumbard had bought a new twenty-foot fishing boat with a huge outboard motor.

Later, at the Sunoco station, someone pointed out Jiggs Blumbard to me. He was in his mid-forties, clean-shaven, below average height. Puffy cheeks and large protruding eyes gave him the innocent look of a crafty old squirrel.

He was filling six five-gallon gas cans in the bed of a Chevy pickup truck. I stood in the doorway with Tim

Meyers, the owner, and watched him. Just to make conversation I said, "Needs gas for his tractor, I suppose."

"Reckon so."

"Pretty late for spring plowing," I hazarded.

"If anybody on that farm does any plowing it'll be the boy. Jiggs is too lazy."

Tim was understandably bitter. He worked six days a week and shared a Ford with his family. Jiggs didn't work at all and owned a Buick and a Honda.

Post Office Box 88 in Fountain had been a dead end for my idea of pot seeds through the mail. I decided to drive down to Jay. After a few miles I realized that Blumbard's pickup was ahead of me.

I slowed down to follow him, an old habit. I watched him turn off on a lane to his right and drive down to a small house. A boy about fourteen came out to unload the truck.

I pulled off on the shoulder to get a look at the Blumbard farm. A small frame house. A lean-to garage. A tractor parked outside the garage. A short distance behind the house was an old barn, badly in need of paint. There was a nice view of the mountains to the south behind the farm.

I drove on; I didn't want to attract attention. Something about the tractor had caught my eye but I wasn't sure what it was.

The post office in Jay was another washout. Box 88 wasn't even rented. I got back on the highway and headed home. On my way I passed the big central school, a long, very modern building. A fleet of twenty buses brought children from all over the district. A large parking lot was jammed with cars. I wondered how many of the kids in school would think growing their own marijuana plants would be a neat thing to do.

Late next morning I drove back to the Blumbard farm. I had to get a closer look at that tractor. When I drove down the lane I saw that Jiggs's truck was gone, probably some minor errand in town. There was no sign of the boy.

The new boat sat on its trailer in front of the house, on display to anyone who passed by, testimony to the Blumbard wealth and social standing.

Years ago I had lost my inhibitions about entering someone's property. If the owner came storming out of his house and demanded to know what I was doing I would simply open my coat and let him see my badge. Then I would look him in the eye and say "police business". That got instant cooperation.

Of course now I don't wear a badge. But I carry a clipboard. If I'm challenged I can say I work for social services. I do investigate fraud cases from time to time, and most people drawing those unemployment or disability checks are afraid not to cooperate.

I opened the gate and walked in. There was a neatly cared-for flower bed by the side of the porch and the yard had been raked. Inside the house a television set was on; I could hear the usual wild audience applause.

A woman came out of the screen door, wiping her hands on her apron. She had to be Mrs. Blumbard. "Can I help you, mister?"

I touched the brim of my hat. "Just want to look at your electric meter, ma'am, thank you."

She was relieved to learn my errand was not important. She nodded and retreated inside. I went around the side of the house where the service drop and the meter were located. From here I had a good view of the tractor.

I was right; something was wrong with the tractor. The front axle was supported by cinder blocks and the left wheel was missing. Tall weeds grew around the large rear wheels. This tractor hadn't been moved for months.

I had seen all I wanted to see. I turned around to go back to my car. The new boat wasn't going near the water anytime soon. The tractor couldn't be driven. Why did Jiggs buy all that gas?

Then I heard a sound, the sound of an engine. Like a chain saw back in the woods but regular and steady. The wind changed and the sound became a bit louder. It was a generator. With electric power right here at the house why would anybody want to run a generator?

When I got home there was a call from Leon. "We got the 88 guy, Uncle Hank. Captain Morris thought you might want to see him. I'll pick you up, okay?"

I was tired but I agreed. Ralph Morris is an old friend. By the time I got the dog fed Leon was at the door in a troop car.

"Remember what the leaflet said?" Leon asked. "Put your money in an 88?"

"I remember. Was it a sedan or a station wagon?"

"Shit!" He stared at me. "How'd you know?"

"I guessed." The printing on the leaflet was sloppy; it had come to me that the phrase "old 88" in the last line was supposed to be "Olds 88". But I shouldn't have spoiled Leon's surprise. "Tell me about it," I said.

"I was nosing around the school and I saw this crowd in the parking lot. There it was, an older model Oldsmobile. And get this—it had pot plants painted all over it. Right! The drawings were pretty wild but you could tell what they were supposed to be.

"Those 'Grow Your Own' leaflets were taped to the windows all around the car. One window was down a few inches and there was a box on the front seat. And get this, Uncle Hank, there was a line of kids shoving envelopes through the window and high-fiving each other. Stupid!

"Anyway there was this guy hanging around and I asked him if it was his car and he said it was and I arrested him."

"What'd you charge him with?"

"Scheming to defraud. The Captain and the D.A. might want to add endangering the welfare of minors. Most of these kids were under eighteen, you know."

Ralph Morris was waiting for us at the satellite station in Keeseville. I live just outside of town and I appreciated being spared the long trip over to headquarters in Ray Brook. The car had been towed in and secured behind a chain link fence.

Morris and I sat at a desk in a small interrogation room. Leon brought in the suspect. His name was Jerry Dunn and he was a student at Clinton Community College. He was a very young man, sandy hair, slight build, with a strangely eager expression.

I know the type. There's a few Jerry Dunns on every campus. They join every debating team in sight and think Thoreau was the greatest brain since Plato.

His face brightened when he saw two older men. He thought he would have an intellectual conversation. He had done something clever and he wanted to be commended.

He was disappointed. Captain Morris barely glanced at him. "What's the charge?" he asked Leon.

"Scheming to defraud and possession of a stolen vehicle."

"A common car thief, eh?" Morris looked disgusted. "Any priors?"

"Checking on that now, sir."

"You find out who the car is registered to?"

43

"A Mr. Edward Franklin, 200 Prospect, Watertown, New York."

Morris turned to me. "What's auto theft now, Henry?"

"One to three years," I said. "This young squirt will probably go to one of the shock camps."

Jerry Dunn looked worried. He hadn't liked being labeled "common" and "squirt".

"Who did that crummy painting on the car?" Morris asked him.

"I did."

Morris made a note. "Criminal mischief."

"Another one to three," I said. "That may get him into Dannemora." I looked at Jerry. "Lots of bad boys in Dannemora."

"Wait a minute!" Jerry said. "I borrowed the car and the paint will come off."

Morris looked skeptical. "That man in Watertown a friend of yours?"

"My cousin, sir."

Morris looked at me. My turn to ask questions.

"You both in this together? This plan to cheat people out of their money?"

"I didn't cheat anybody!" Jerry insisted. "I didn't!"

"You took those kids' money, didn't you?"

"No, sir. They just put their money in the box on the front seat. There was no intent to defraud..." He wanted to make a speech but I cut him off.

"Just another cheap con," I said. "Why didn't you throw in some gold mine stock?" I pushed back my chair. "Lock him up."

Jerry Dunn was disappointed. Nobody had said his scheme was original, nobody had thought he was smart. And he was getting scared.

Captain Morris nodded. "Hold him for the judge."

"Wait a minute!" Jerry looked from me to Morris and back again. "I'm writing a paper for school. This was an exercise in applied psychology. You know, the power of suggestion, of group mind sets. It's my own project."

I looked at him. "Whose class are you in?" I asked him.

"Dr. Edwin Mimms." Leon left the room.

"Tell me about this cousin of yours. Is he a college student, too?"

"Er, no. He's in business."

"What kind of business?"

"He works for his father."

In a minute Leon was back. "There is a Dr. Mimms at the college. He teaches psychology."

"Too bad he doesn't teach a class in staying out of jail," Morris said. "Lock up this young man, officer."

"Wait a minute," I said. Jerry looked at me as if I held a last-minute reprieve.

"Jerry, you and your cousin Eddie were in this to-gether, weren't you? You never intended to mail out any seeds, did you?" I was fishing, but there had been a lot of drug activity in Watertown.

Jerry gave me a grateful look and shook his head.

"Eddie's a pusher, right? You wanted material for your paper and Eddie wanted a prospect list for his pot sales. Eddie wants to sell pot around the high school and you helped him."

Jerry stared at the floor and nodded. There was a long silence.

"Where's Eddie now?" Morris asked. Jerry gave him an address. "Put him away."

Leon took Jerry Dunn's arm to lead him out.

"Sir?" Jerry said to me. I turned around. "I'm still going to write that paper," he said.

"You do that," I said. "I think you'll do a fine job."

"Thank you, sir." He was smiling as Leon led him away.

On the way home I recalled what an old sheriff told me one time: "People stay up nights figuring out new ways to break the law. There's a new way every day."

"And there's more of them than of us," I said.

"Yes, but we're smarter than they are," he said. "We have to be."

I went to bed early. Tomorrow I was going to visit the Blumbard farm again.

"All right, you guys, you know the drill. Watch for trip wires. Roberts, you take the left side of the barn and secure that generator. Sessions, you stay behind me. You copy?"

"Understood."

There were six men in the raiding party, including a top sergeant who wasn't fond of civilians getting in his way. His detail had been on search missions like this before. I was included as an observer.

Three of us took the path that led to the door of the little barn; the other men fanned out and approached slowly through the high grass and weeds. The sun was hot and there was no breeze.

This was a joint operation between the State Police Narcotics Unit and the Guard Counterdrug Detachment. We had descended on the Blumbard place in mid-morning. The dooryard was crowded with dark blue police cars and multi-hued personnel carriers. Jiggs and his family were being detained on the front porch by a polite officer. Up on the highway a trooper kept curious traffic moving.

The old barn looked totally deserted. The one window on the side facing us had been boarded up. We could hear the even pounding of the generator. Again I told myself that I could be wrong; that there could be some innocent reason why an old barn was giving off those waves of heat that could be picked up by a snooping helicopter.

"Hold it!" a man on my right said suddenly. "We got something."

The sergeant snapped a look back at me. "Freeze, pop." He stepped back a few paces and then over to join the man.

It was a trip wire, a length of fishing line stretched at ankle height. Carefully the man who had spotted it traced it to a corner of the barn. The line ran up through eye hooks to a shotgun fastened under the eave. A careless step would have pulled the trigger. The gun would have fired into the air, but it would have scared the heck out of a casual prowler.

Ten minutes later we were at the door. It was secured by a heavy padlock. Blumbard had surrendered the key to us after a trooper handed him the search warrant. A soldier named Sweeney checked the door frame for traps and opened the door.

We crowded inside and stood there silently. The interior was a greenhouse and it was filled with lush marijuana plants. It was hot and humid and rank with the smell. And it was brighter than daylight with a dozen or more huge floodlights hanging from the ceiling like small suns.

"Kill some of those lights," the sergeant ordered, "and get that window open."

The plants were growing in long tin trays placed on low wooden tables. They were all at least five feet high, with rich, glossy leaves. There was a tangle of garden hoses and sacks of what must have been a plant nutrient. Along one wall was a nursery; two hundred or more seedling plants were growing in old washtubs. A pile of dried stalks was in a corner; the leaves must have been harvested every week or so this summer.

Beside me the sarge cleared his throat. "Sweeney, get the camera. The major won't believe this."

For the next two hours there was considerable traffic in and around the barn and farm. The county sheriff came over from E'town. A BCI officer came over from Ray Brook. A Channel Five news team shot a lot of tape. An FBI agent and a DEA man from Plattsburgh dropped in. We all had the same thought: a little cottage industry was getting much more sophisticated.

Finally the sergeant said, "All right. Party's over. Pull 'em up and we'll take 'em away."

"Wait," I said. "Count the plants first. The mature ones." The law up here says the county can confiscate the property of anyone caught growing more than one hundred pot plants.

He looked at me. "Some reason, pop?"

"Just do it, all right?"

He went down one side and I took the other. We met in the center.

"I make it a hundred and sixty-four," I said.

"That's what I got," the sarge said. "You happy now, pop?"

"Yes, thanks." He turned away. I let him take three or four steps. "Sergeant!"

He looked back, surprised.

"It's Deputy Sessions when you speak to me. You copy?"

"Yes, sir."

Age, like rank, hath its privileges. I went out to catch a ride home.

Jiggs Blumbard had enjoyed all the attention and excitement. But when he realized he was being arrested on felony charges, Jiggs named his brother-in-law as chief gardener.

It was the brother-in-law who had been afraid that high consumption of electricity by a tiny farmhouse would attract attention. It was the brother-in-law who assured Jiggs the strange plants in the barn were sugar cane. His only job, Jiggs insisted, was to keep the generator fueled.

With Jiggs Blumbard in jail maybe I could do something about getting his son back in school. With a parent like his the boy would need all the education he could get.

Two days later I was on my porch after lunch. I had been on the phone with the sergeant in charge of that Guard detail; his name was Matt Bennett.

We'd talked a couple of times since our raid on the barn. He called to tell me that Blumbard's brother-in-law was in custody. Along with a van load of marijuana leaves and buds ready for market.

"Fifty pounds or more," Matt said. "Worth about a hundred thousand on the street."

"A Class C felony," I said, "good for fifteen years even without intent to sell."

Matt and I have a ten-dollar bet on the outcome of the case. He thinks a smart defense lawyer will claim that our helicopter reconnaissance was an invasion of privacy and have our search warrant thrown out. I'm betting that doesn't happen but I've been wrong before.

I was thinking of taking a nap when Leon phoned.

"Here's a new scheme, Uncle Hank. It's a small ad in the paper. It says: 'Be a farmer. We will lease you a square yard of ground. Plant anything you want to! We do the watering and keep the deer away. Free use of tools and no questions asked. When your friends ask you can say you grow your own.'

"There's a phone number. You want to check it out with us, Uncle Hank?"

"No, Leon," I said. "You boys handle it. I'll wait for the next one."

A Feeling for the Truth

Southbound traffic from Canada into New York was usually light on Friday afternoons. Only four of the seven Customs booths at the border were manned. For Inspector Cass Gilbert, the work had been routine; she had passed through Canadians bound for a weekend of shopping in Plattsburgh and several New York residents returning from day trips to Montreal. They were legitimate citizens on legitimate errands. But Cass, who was twenty-eight and had been in Customs for two years, knew there were always some people intent on evading the law.

From her glass-enclosed booth she could see for miles in every direction. The Champlain Port of Entry was set on a broad treeless plain; its complex of severely functional buildings housed Customs, Immigration, the Border Patrol, and various law agencies. A few yards up the highway was their counterpart, a Canadian station that handled traffic crossing into Canada. Both installations flanked New York Interstate 87, the superhighway from Albany to Montreal.

Cass watched as a big Cadillac slid noiselessly to a stop outside her booth. Automatically she noted the occupants: a couple in the front seat, both past middle age, well dressed, man driving. One child in the rear, strapped into a car seat and surrounded by stuffed toys. Vermont plates on the car.

Cass's first questions were standard: "Where were you born? Where do you live?" (A Customs inspector's initial duty was to establish nationality and citizenship.) Then, "How long were you in Canada?" Satisfied with the answers, Cass asked, "Anything to declare? Anything you bought in Canada?"

The wife leaned across the seat, smiling, anxious to be helpful. She gestured toward the little girl. "Only a new Barney for our granddaughter." To the child she said, "You love Barney, don't you, dear?"

The child clutched the purple dinosaur and nodded shyly.

"And Barney loves you, doesn't he?"

The child nodded again. "Barney loves me," she murmured.

The woman beamed at Cass. "Isn't she the cutest thing?"

Cass gave her a brief smile. She looked at the husband: paunchy, fraternal rings, salesman's smile. "Anything else?" she asked.

He shook his head, grinning broadly. "We hit a lot of restaurants; I put on about ten pounds," he laughed. "I bought a couple of shirts. Nothing to declare."

Not likely, Cass thought. Three days in Montreal and nothing to declare? Shoppers from the States went to Montreal to take advantage of a favorable exchange rate that made the U.S. dollar worth much more than the Canadian dollar. These people obviously had money and liked to spend it. Cass made a decision.

"Drive down there, please." She pointed to the secondary Customs inspection area.

"What for?" The smiles disappeared from both faces. "What for?"

Swiftly she made notes on a printed slip and put it under the car's windshield wiper.

"Drive down there, sir, for a secondary inspection."

The man began to bluster. "Look here, young lady, our taxes pay your salary..."

"Please move on, sir, you're blocking traffic," Cass said. (First rule for inspectors handling the public: be polite.)

She stepped back. The man growled something and put the big car in gear. At the secondary inspection station her request would have the car thoroughly checked—the trunk, the interior, the luggage.

Cass frowned as she watched the Cadillac move away. The woman had been pushy, the man patronizing, but there had been nothing overtly suspicious. She had acted on a hunch. She had been assigned to Passenger Traffic for just over a week; maybe she'd been too hasty.

"This job calls for a lot of snap judgments," Cass had said to her friend and supervisor, Sam Barry. "What do we have to go on? Instinct, common sense, body language, hunches?"

Sam grinned. "All of the above," he said. "Just call it a feeling for the truth."

Cass looked beyond the passenger traffic lanes at the commercial lanes to the west. That was where the big trucks and cargo carriers had to stop for inspection. She had been assigned to Commercial for a year. That's where the action is, she thought.

Customs is a branch of Treasury, charged with collecting revenue due Uncle Sam. This brings Customs head-to-head with smugglers, traffickers in anything with resale value: armaments, narcotics, currency, even people.

To Cass, the work on the commercial side had been exciting and rewarding. Bills of lading and cargo declarations were carefully checked and spot checks made. A load of lumber billed as pine had been found to be much more valuable black walnut. A scanning device had detected fifty slot machines under a load of mattresses. A load of furniture weighed more than it should have because of the cases of assault rifles hidden under false flooring.

The intercom in her booth sounded. It was Carter Kelso, one of the inspectors working the secondary position this afternoon. Carter was a classmate; Cass had met him during the eleven-week course at the Law Enforcement Training Center in Glynco, Georgia. He was reporting on the Cadillac that Cass had sent over.

"Good call," he said. "The dame had a new fur coat in the trunk, still in the box."

"How about <u>those</u> stuffed toys in the back seat?" she asked.

"There's a pink rabbit with a diamond ring sewed up in its tummy," Carter told her. A skilled appraiser would present the Cadillac owners with a statement of duty owed.

"Thanks, Carter," Cass said.

"Any time." The intercom went off.

Sam, her supervisor, had walked up quietly and stood outside her booth. "Carter told me you scored," he said. "That make you feel better about this assignment?"

Sam was the only person on the station who knew her first name was actually Cassandra, and he had kept it a secret. Cass knew she could confide in him.

"Of course I'm glad we nailed them," she said, "but the last day I was in Commercial we short-stopped three missile launchers waybilled as agricultural machinery. Over here some rich dame tries to sneak in a fur coat, or some guy hides a watch in his shoe." She shrugged. "It's quite a change of pace."

"Seems pretty penny ante?" asked Sam.

She gave him a smile. "Sometimes."

"Maybe you'll change your mind."

Toward six o'clock the stream of cars quickened. It was early spring, but dusk was approaching. There was a glow in the sky from the little town of Champlain two miles distant. Three cars were waiting in line, but Cass was concentrating on the one outside her booth. She suspected it had been stolen. It was an almost new Chevrolet four-door sedan in a bright pastel color, a model she knew to be favored by professional car thieves. Cars stolen in Canada were often driven to Delaware or Pennsylvania for shipment overseas.

The driver had been a shade too ready with his answers. He was French-Canadian, young, clean-shaven, wearing the usual black leather jacket. His license said he was Pascal Favreau of Brossard, Quebec. There were two men in the back seat. Stolen cars didn't usually carry passengers, but they could be clever window dressing.

A light blinked on the screen in the booth, and the computer confirmed her hunch; the car was stolen. The driver was smiling at Cass, unaware that his license had been scanned electronically and the state police alerted.

"These are my oncles," he said, pointing at the men in the rear seat. "They have been visiting my mother. They live in Pittsburgh. I take them to the train in Al-

bany." He reached for the ignition key. "I go now, ma-
dame?"

"Not yet." Cass looked at the two men. They were
both middle-aged, dressed in shabby suits with shirts
and ties. To the nearer man Cass said, "Where were you
born, sir?"

"They are born in Canada," the driver cut in, "and
now they live..."

Cass silenced him with a wave of her hand. "They
have to answer for themselves." She tried again.
"Where were you born?"

The men were both smiling and nodding at her.
"Peetsborg," they chorused, "Peetsborg."

There are foreign nationals who work in the States,
Cass reminded herself, and some of them don't speak
English very well. Most of them, however, don't ride
around in stolen cars. These must be a couple of aliens,
she decided. Probably gave this kid every cent they had
to bring them across.

She signaled for an INS team. Let Immigration
make the decision, check for working papers, criminal
records, establish nationality. She hit the switch that
changed the traffic light above her booth from green
to red.

"My oncles do not speak so well," the driver offered.
He saw the INS team approaching and turned to Cass
in alarm. "We can go now? I take them to Albany."

The two agents from Immigration and Naturalization stood by the side of the car. Both men wore
sidearms. "Step out of the car, please."

The driver turned to Cass in desperation. "How
about if I leave them here and come back for them?"

"No," Cass said politely. "You have to go with these
men."

The driver looked back sorrowfully as he and the two men were led away. A man came to take the Chevrolet to a garage where it would be checked by a detail of the New York State Auto Theft Unit.

Cass recalled the time when she and another inspector in Commercial had checked out a tanker truck. Instead of fifty thousand gallons of fuel oil, it contained forty almost suffocated aliens from Turkey. She had no doubt that these two would be denied admission and detained.

"Right," Sam said later, "and that kid Favreau was arrested. The Montreal Urban Police want him."

"Why would he try to bring aliens across in a stolen car?" Cass asked.

"Way I see it," Sam answered, "he was moonlighting, trying to pick up some extra bucks. He's hired to drive the stolen car across, probably to some transfer point like Glens Falls, where he takes Amtrak back to Montreal. But he contracts with some other people to bring across a couple of illegals. And he got nailed."

Cass shook her head. "A dumb thing to do."

Sam grinned at her. "Be thankful for the stupid ones. They make our job easier."

It was dark when the dog show man appeared, on his way home from somewhere in Ontario. Cass had passed him through northbound two days ago and had been hoping to see him again. He was a big man, overweight, balding, driving a Mercury station wagon.

The rear of the wagon was taken up by a large dog cage. The back seat was folded down, and the space was filled with sacks of feed, blankets, water jugs, and other gear. A velour banner with gold letters reading SUNSET KENNEL was draped over the top of the cage. Several blue ribbons were pinned to the banner.

"How-do, officer," said the man. He had stepped out of the car, and Cass noticed again that he was dressed in riding pants with highly polished boots, a checkered vest, and an ascot tie.

Cass remembered his name. "Evening, Mr. Atkins. How's Queenie?"

"Never better, thanks."

Queenie was a female golden retriever. When she heard Cass's voice, she sat up in her cage and whined. Cass stepped to the rear window and put her hand through to the side of the cage. Queenie sniffed at it and wagged her tail. "Hello, pretty girl," said Cass softly. She scratched the dog under her chin, avoiding the sharp bristles on her muzzle, and stroked her shaggy ears.

For the convenience of the Canadian inspectors the dog's rabies vaccination certificate was in a plastic holder taped to the inside of the window. The dog's formal name was Elizabeth Tudor the Third.

"How was the show?" Cass asked.

"Queenie did it again," the man said proudly. "Took Best of Show." He held up a colorful ribbon for Cass to see. "There's another little do in Pointe Claire tomorrow," he said. "Maybe we can make it a double-header this week."

Cass had learned that he took the dog to a show almost every week. "Large or small, we hit 'em all," the man had told her. "I'm retired, nothing better to do. But we do have fun, don't we, Queenie girl?"

Cass waved him on. The dog's soulful brown eyes watched her as the wagon pulled away. "Poor dog," Cass said.

She punched a button on the intercom. "Sam, remember the dog show man I told you about? He just went through, and now I'm sure he's dirty."

Sam's voice was calm. "I hope you're right, Cass. We'll let Smith decide what to do." Two minutes later he called back. "Smith's office, seven o'clock."

The director's office was small and dominated by a large desk holding a computer and several scanning screens. White-haired and dignified, Courtland Smith looked more like a minister than the director of one of the nation's busiest ports of entry.

"Is there any physical evidence that this man is transporting narcotics?" asked Director Smith.

"No, sir."

Cass stood in front of the desk, Sam a pace behind her. Also in the room were Dale Handford, a plain-clothes Customs agent, and a DEA agent named Matt Riley. Cass knew what the director could be thinking: here's a young inspector, just transferred to Passenger Traffic, seeing a smuggler in every car. It had happened before.

"Suspicious circumstances," offered Sam, backing her up.

Dale Handford spoke up. "Officer Gilbert brought this to my attention a couple of days ago. A man taking a dog to a kennel show in Canada could give himself almost perfect cover for transporting narcotics."

Smith nodded. "You say he makes a trip across every week?"

"Sometimes twice a week," Sam answered.

"But how many dog shows can there be in Canada?" asked Riley, the DEA man.

"It wouldn't have to be a sanctioned show," Cass told him. "There's always a neighborhood show, or a charity event, in the papers. But I think that's just his cover." All he has to do is know how to talk about them. He may not go anywhere near a dog show."

Smith nodded again. "Inspector Gilbert, exactly what makes you think this man is not entering his dog in a kennel show somewhere?"

Cass took a deep breath. Sam and Agent Handford had heard her idea before, but this would be new to Director Smith. She looked at him squarely.

"Because the dog's ears aren't trimmed right."

Behind her she heard what might have been a laugh from Matt Riley, but she went on. "On a dog like that, the hair above the ears should be trimmed down. It doesn't hurt, and it makes the dog's ears look lower. Judges like that. And the muzzle should be clipped. That hasn't been done, either."

She paused. Everybody in the room was looking at her. Cass gestured at Sam and Agent Handford. "We discussed this two days ago, but we decided that the grooming, or lack of it, was an oversight, something the owner would take care of before the next show."

She took another deep breath. "The owner, this man Atkins, passed through tonight and told me he had just won a Best of Show." She paused again. "There's no way that dog could have taken a Best of Show in even a small affair. Not with those ears."

She stopped. Nobody said anything; they were all looking at Director Smith.

He gave Cass a brief smile and looked around the office. "I'll buy that," he said mildly. "Now the question is, what do we do about it?" He glanced at Riley. "Matt, how are you fixed for manpower?"

Cass knew what he meant. They could apprehend the dog show man here and shake down his vehicle. But if they found any contraband, as Cass thought they would, they would forfeit the chance of locating the man's contacts in Canada. If Riley could detail a DEA team to work with the Canadians and follow Atkins, they would have a shot at breaking up the distribution ring.

"We can get right on it," Riley said. "Sam, have your people point this guy out, and we'll handle it with our friends up the road. No sweat."

Cass said, "Atkins mentioned another show tomorrow. He may cross again in the morning."

Dale Handford had a thought. "If this is part of the cocaine pipeline from Florida, they could be working the same dodge somewhere else. The Buffalo district, maybe."

"Good point," said Director Smith. "Anything else?"

"One thing," Cass said hesitantly, "be careful with the dog. He probably keeps the poor thing tranquilized."

"We'll be careful," said Riley.

The meeting was over; the men filed out the door. Director Smith held out his hand to Cass. "Thanks, inspector," he said. "By the way, my daughter-in-law shows cocker spaniels. She's very fussy about their ears."

When her shift was over Cass went home to a beagle named Kelly and a partially finished paper for her college sociology class. As she played with the puppy she thought about the forlorn look in Queenie's brown eyes. "Be glad you're not in show business, fella," she said to Kelly.

The next day, Saturday, Cass and a shift of inspectors would work the northbound traffic. The briefing this morning was on the familiar subject of narcotics. "As you know," a Customs agent told them, "there's a steady stream of cocaine flowing north into Canada from Florida. Payment comes back down in the form of good U.S. currency. The DEA says heroin is becoming the drug of choice in some big cities. Nigeria has learned the tricks of the trade from Colombia. Our informants tell us there's a big push on untaxed liquor going into Canada through our smaller ports. Good luck this weekend."

Right, thought Cass as she walked out to her booth. With any luck at all, we'll nail Atkins; he'll be hard to miss with all of us watching for him. She thought again of Queenie. "Poor dog," she whispered.

"Whooie, look what we got here!" A man was grinning at her from the window of a van. Another man sat beside him. "A little girl all dressed up in a u-nee-form!"

The driver was leering at her, hoping for some reaction. She saw the passenger pull at the driver's sleeve. "Cool it, Jerry," he muttered. "We're in a hurry."

Cass gritted her teeth. Here was another stone-age relic, one of the few remaining males who couldn't accept the notion of a woman in authority. First rule, be polite.

"Where were you born? Where do you live?" Cass asked pleasantly.

"New York," answered the passenger.

"What's it to you, honey?" answered the driver.

The van was old, with faded paint and rust showing along the fender seams. On the side was lettered the name of a painting contractor with a Syracuse address. Both men wore workclothes.

Cass faced the driver. "Where are you heading in Canada?"

"Got a couple of kitchen painting jobs in Napierville," the driver answered. "Now you be careful not to hurt yourself with that pretty little gun you're wearing," he said with exaggerated concern.

Cass ignored him. She rapped on the side of the van. "Let's take a look inside."

"Sure thing, little lady."

The driver stepped out and walked back to the rear of the van. He was a big man with thinning brown hair and overdeveloped biceps displayed by a tight shirt. He opened the single wide door. "Help yourself."

Cass stood in the opening and looked inside. There was a strong smell of paint thinner. She saw a jumble of painting gear, dropcloths, an extension ladder, a box that held brushes. There was a gallon of oil-based white primer on the floor, and there were three new cases of primer against the wall. She saw two worn and scuffed suitcases on the floor in the front. Cass picked up the can of primer and read the label. It was a nationally known brand. The three cases against the wall were the same product.

"Lots of primer to paint a kitchen," she said.

"Oh yeah," the driver said, stepping close to her. "It was on sale, so I stocked up. I always use primer when I paint, then whatever color the lady of the house wants." He gave her a leering smile. "I always give the lady what she wants."

Disgusted, Cass stepped away. His partner had said they were in a hurry. "How would you feel about unloading all this stuff for us," she asked, "so we can take a nice long look?" That ought to jerk a knot in his tail, she thought.

The man straightened, a look of consternation on his face. "Now look, lady, it's all just painting stuff." The leering expression was gone. "I got a schedule to keep."

He glanced around; there was nobody in sight. He reached into a pocket. "How about I just hand you this and you let me be on my way. All right?" He held out a folded hundred-dollar bill.

Cass was not surprised at the offer of a bribe, but she was surprised at the amount of it; she would have expected it to be no more than a twenty.

"No, thanks," she said. "How about you drive down there," she pointed. "Right now."

"I didn't mean anything, honest."

"Right now!" Cass slapped the form on his windshield, noting that the helper was now behind the wheel. He drove to the inspection area, his big-mouth partner sitting silently at his side.

Cass got Carter on the intercom. "The big sucker in the van tried to buy me with a C-note. Could be counterfeit."

"I'll check."

Paint and brushes don't make a painter, Cass told herself; there's something wrong with that van. Maybe Carter will find it.

In half an hour Carter called back. "Macho Man has twelve of those hundreds on him. His partner has six. All genuine currency. Everything else seems legit. You want to press a charge of bribery, Cass?"

"Wouldn't stick," Cass answered. "He would just deny it. But hold on, Carter, I've got to have another look."

She called Sam. "All right if I close down for a few minutes? Got a problem at the garage."

"Go ahead."

She switched the traffic light to red, closed her booth, and started for the inspection garage. From the corner of her eye she saw a Mercury station wagon pulling away from the booth on the end. It was the dog show man, on his way again.

There was nothing she could do now; Riley's men and the Canadian police would follow him. In an hour he could be in Montreal. Or he might be at a dog show, and Cass would have caused a lot of manpower to be wasted.

The paint van stood in one of the bays, flanked by long tables on either side. The van's contents had been placed on the floor and the tables for examination. The driver and his helper stood against a wall some distance away under the watchful eye of a Customs agent.

"We checked the spare tire and the usual places," Carter told her, "and we had one of the dogs in, but he couldn't do much against the paint smell. You think we ought to pull up the floor?"

Cass shook her head. "No, it's something I saw." Her eye fell on the extension ladder, now leaning against a table.

"That's it," she said to Carter. "There's no stepladder. You don't paint a kitchen without a stepladder. And those brushes; they shouldn't be thrown together in a box. And there's no small brush for trim painting."

"So they do sloppy work," said Carter, puzzled. "You got anything else?"

The gallon of primer was on the table. Cass picked it up and looked at it. The lid was clean and smooth; it had not been opened. She looked around, frowning.

The three cases of primer were now on the floor. They had been opened and the overhead lights reflected off the tops of four new gallon cans in each box.

Carter saw Cass staring at the cases of paint. He lifted out one of the cans and handed it to her. "Look," he said, "same label, 'Five Star Sealer Primer,' same thing you've got there."

Cass was holding one can in each hand. Suddenly she looked at Carter, her eyes shining. "Except for one thing," she said. She handed the cans to Carter. He hefted them slowly. "Yeah," he said, "this can seems a touch lighter."

It was the can from the floor of the van. "Right," Cass said. "Does that tell us anything?"

"That this can is not quite as full as the other one."

"Maybe." A tiny suspicion was growing in her mind. "Only one way to find out. Open it."

Carter hesitated.

"Go ahead, Carter! Open it!"

He spread a piece of canvas on the table and placed each can on it. Carefully he pried off the lid of the lighter can. They bent closer to see the contents. The can was full of smooth white paint.

Now Carter was suspicious. He turned to the second can and opened it. It was also brimful of white paint. He looked at Cass. "Maybe we were wrong."

She shook her head. "Not yet, buddy!" She snatched up a long-bladed screwdriver from a toolbox and stuck it into the paint. With Carter watching she moved it in a circle. The blade stopped against something below the surface of the paint, something solid.

Cass looked at Carter, her eyes wide with excitement. "Bingo," she said softly.

"Bingo," he echoed. He brought a waste can out from under the table. Holding the can with both hands, he carefully poured out the white liquid. The tops of two bricklike shapes emerged from the paint.

Cass lifted one out and Carter swabbed it clean with paper towels. It was a brick of cocaine, carefully sealed in plastic. Carter examined it. "See that little red mark?" he said. "They put that on down in Colombia. This stuff must be as pure as it comes."

He signaled to the agent in charge of the two men. "Arrest them. Possession." As the agent led them away, the driver jerked his arm free and looked at Cass.

"Officer, I guess I never should have come on to you like I did."

Cass detected a note of apology in his voice. She bit back the remarks she might have made to him. "You got that right, junior," she said.

Carter and his crew were busy with the cases of primer. Each of the twelve gallons was found to hold two four-pound bricks of cocaine.

Cass shook her head. "All we've got them on is possession of a controlled substance. We can't make a case of intent to distribute. That big sucker was just an errand boy."

"Don't worry," Carter told her. "To the kingpins down in Florida or wherever, he blew the delivery. It's his fault they lost several million dollars' worth of merchandise. They won't forget that when he gets out."

Traffic was light when Cass returned to her booth. She hit the intercom for Sam's station. "Any word from Riley and the Mounties?"

"Not yet. Patience, my girl."

"Yes, boss."

An hour passed during which Cass cleared a number of early summer vacationers bound for Ontario and Quebec. She politely explained that she did not supply road maps or recommend accommodations. And she worried. More than enough time had elapsed for Atkins to reach Montreal. Maybe he had actually gone to a dog show. If so, Riley would have a new shaggy dog story to tell the station.

A pickup truck braked to a stop outside the booth, and a voice said, "Shake it up, kid, I haven't got all day."

The driver was a man dressed in a checked flannel shirt and jeans. He wore a mechanic's cap with a John Deere emblem. A second man sat in the passenger seat. The truck was a new model with extra chrome trim and a row of spotlights on the roof. No name on the door. New York plates.

A deer rifle was suspended across the rear window of the cab. A rifle in a truck window is a common status symbol in northern New York, but it is not to be casually taken across the border.

Cass faced the driver. "Are you planning to take that gun into Canada with you, sir?"

"What do you think?" he answered. "It's my truck and my gun. Sure I am."

"I'm sorry, sir, but it's illegal."

"Now look, sister," the driver said arrogantly, "this ain't no concealed weapon, and I got my rights!"

This is my day for weirdos, Cass thought. Doggedly she continued. "If you're going on a hunting trip, you have to have a Form CF 4455 in your possession."

The driver shook his head and sneered. "No, I ain't going hunting, 'cept in a few bars." His passenger snickered. "And I ain't got a form whatever."

"I'm sorry, but it's illegal for you to transport that firearm ..."

The driver interrupted again. "No prissy-ass girl is going to tell me what to do." His passenger snickered again. "And you better believe it."

Cass stepped out of the booth and walked to the rear of the truck. First rule, be polite, even to redneck bullies. The bed of the truck was empty; no luggage equalled no hunting. She noted the bumper sticker: THIS VEHICLE INSURED BY SMITH AND WESSON. She went back to the driver's side.

"I'm sorry, sir, but I can't let you proceed with that firearm in your possession. You'll have to..."

"By God, that's about all I'm going to listen to, you—" He added some words Cass had rarely heard. She had had enough. She slammed her fist into the side of the door; the loud bang shocked the man into silence.

"Now, listen, you boneheaded bastard," she said sternly. "You get this crap bucket turned around and the hell out of here before I throw your sorry ass in jail, you hear me?"

The man's mouth hung open. He gulped once. His passenger pulled at his sleeve. "Let's go! Let's go!" he whispered.

"You hear me?" Cass demanded in a loud voice.

"Yes."

"Yes what?" Still louder.

"Yes, ma'am."

"Now, move it!"

The driver put the truck in reverse, cautiously made a U-turn, and was gone.

The intercom, Cass thought suddenly, did I leave the intercom open? Could somebody have heard me?

She spun around to check and almost ran into Director Smith. He and Sam stood on the curb.

Cass sagged against the door frame. "I'm sorry you had to hear that, sir," she said.

The two men glanced at each other. "Hear what?" Smith asked in a mild tone. "I didn't hear anything."

Sam was grinning at her. "We just came to tell you that Atkins, the dog show man, is under arrest. His station wagon was loaded with narcotics. You were right, Cass."

She felt weak with relief. "Thanks," she said. "Thanks."

Director Smith supplied the details. "The surveillance team trailed the subject to a residential area near Mirabel Airport. Several parties were waiting for him in a large garage. They are all now in custody. The man

Atkins is smart enough to waive extradition. He's supplying the DEA with details of the operation."

Smith held out his hand. "Congratulations, Inspector Gilbert."

"Thank you, sir."

"One more thing. The subject's vehicle and its contents were confiscated, of course. It appears that the dog was stolen somewhere downstate. Naturally we'll try to locate its owner, but in the meantime we should find a home for it. Do you think you could help us out?"

Queenie was safe; it was what Cass had been hoping to hear. "Yes, sir. No trouble at all. Be glad to."

Smith nodded gravely. He turned and walked back to the administration building. Cass was overjoyed. Queenie would get along just fine with Kelly. Maybe there was an owner still out there and maybe not, but for now Queenie would have a home again.

Sam touched her arm. "The dog is waiting for you over in the garage. Go on over and say hello; I'll take over here for you."

"Thanks, Sam." She turned to go.

"Just a minute, Cass." Sam's tone was serious. "If you want to transfer back to Commercial, I can arrange it."

"Not on your life, boss. I'm beginning to like it here."

The Bust of the Year

At first I didn't believe John T about the cocaine. Not that I thought he was lying, we've been friends too long for that. I thought someone was conning him.

"Did you hear me, Hank? The car was just sitting there in the parking lot with eighty-four pounds of cocaine in the trunk."

John T has too many years in with the Bureau to be easily fooled, and he never sounds excited like this on the phone.

"I heard you, John T." I answered. "You mean the driver just left it and walked away?"

"Right. A DEA agent was tailing him. The guy parked right in front of the Beef Palace restaurant in Ogdensburg and took off. Disappeared!"

"Does the agent know who the driver was?" I asked.

"It was one of Little Augie Vanvetti's men, from the Florida family. Hank, that much coke would be worth over five million on the street."

Even I knew who Augie Vanvetti was. He and his family ran a big cocaine pipeline from Miami and West

Palm into Montreal. "Wait a minute, John T," I said. "Why didn't somebody follow the driver?"

"It was this way, Hank. The DEA man was alone. He had been tailing the car all day, and he figured the driver was going into the restaurant for something to eat. So he went to a phone to call his office. When he got back, the driver was gone."

That's the breaks you get in law enforcement; I know, I was there myself once. "I don't see your problem, John T. Just have somebody sit on the car until the driver or someone else comes back to pick it up."

There was a pause; I heard John T take a deep breath. "The car's gone, Hank. It got towed away." That news item made me take a deep breath, too. So now the car had disappeared?

John T kept talking. "The DEA's got it in a garage on Route 37, Slater's Mobil, two miles south of the Ogdensburg Interchange. Get over there, Hank. That car is a hot lead to Vanvetti; don't let anybody screw it up. This could be the drug bust of the year, old buddy."

It sounded to me like the operation was already screwed up. "I dunno, John T. Pheasant season opens in three days and I've..."

"Just give me one day, Hank. Two days, tops. Check in with Newt Owens; he's a friend of yours."

He was right there, Newt is a friend of mine. "All right," I said. "Two days."

John T is John T. Farley, section chief of the FBI office in Syracuse. I'm Hank Sessions, retired deputy sheriff and sometime fishing and hunting guide. He and I did a hitch in the military police four wars back. He calls me when something goes off the track up here in what he calls my back yard.

Like now. The DEA had practically stumbled across a car full of cocaine that might belong to Augustus Vanvetti. Little Augie is on a trip north here, and the Drug Enforcement Administration is tailing him, hoping to get a line on his local contacts and maybe catch him with some of the family merchandise.

And since northern New York is his turf, John T has politely extended the services of his office. And now he was about to offer mine as well.

"It looks like Little Augie has made a colossal mistake," John T said happily. "Really big."

His call had caught me in Potsdam, away from my home base in Keeseville. It took me five minutes to get on the road; Ogdensburg was about an hour to the west on the St. Lawrence Seaway. John T had given me some more background details.

A downstate DEA team had picked up Little Augie and his men in Lake George. Augie was driving himself in a big new Cadillac. One of his men was driving a late model Lincoln Continental, and a third man was in a Honda. All three cars had out-of-state tags.

A room is waiting for him at the Holiday Inn. Augie goes in, leaving one man outside to watch the cars. One agent stakes out the motel room, leaving the other, a man named Bill Clark, downstairs. Pretty soon Augie comes out with a man the agent has never seen before. They exchange a few words, and the stranger gets into the Lincoln. Augie gives him a wave as he drives away.

Bill Clark, the DEA street agent, figures the man is just running an errand, but he follows him. He is surprised to see the man head for Interstate 87 and drive north. Clark has no choice, he follows the Lincoln. Meanwhile, Little Augie disappears. He ducks out a back door or something, jumps in his car, and is gone.

That's how it happened that about three-thirty this afternoon a big Lincoln with a fortune in the trunk is left unattended outside the Beef Palace restaurant, parked in a Handicapped Only space. Obviously some-body is supposed to pick it up. But who, and why the delay?

"Wherever he is, Little Augie must be sweating bul-lets," John T said. His car and his cocaine have van-ished. Did somebody sell him out? Is somebody trying to take over his business?

Anyway, there's Bill Clark, watching the big Lincoln. He has lost the driver; he isn't about to lose the car. He has checked the doors, they are locked. There's noth-ing visible inside but an innocent road map on the front seat. He has checked the license with his office; the car has not been reported stolen. He learns that Little Augie has given his teammate the slip. By late afternoon Clark thinks the car has simply been abandoned. But it is a connection with Little Augie, and he has been told to stick with it, so he does.

About then the manager of the Beef Palace takes a hand. He resents the rudeness and discourtesy of peo-ple who take the handicapped parking spaces because they are closer, and some of his customers have com-plained about the big car by his front door.

So the manager canvasses the tables and checks the men's room; nobody belongs to the big car. The man-ager phones the police to complain about an illegally parked car, and he calls a garage to come and take the car away.

Bill Clark watches as a tow truck comes and jockeys the Lincoln out of the parking lot and hauls it to a garage nearby. He follows and identifies himself to the owner, a man named Buck Slater. Clark has him put the Lincoln out of sight behind the garage. A state trooper arrives and confirms that the car is not on a stolen list.

Now Bill Clark has a hunch. There might be some-thing in the car that would indicate Little Augie's present whereabouts, or at least justify all the time he has put in on this job. He decides he has sufficient probable cause to open the car and take a look inside.

"He may have been wrong about that," John T told me, "But nobody was there to argue the point."

Buck Slater, the garage man, helped Clark with the door lock. "Part of my job," he explained. "I get calls all the time, people lock themselves out."

There was nothing of interest under the seats or in the glovebox. The trunk was something else again. It was crammed with camping gear, all brand-new: a small tent, a folding stove, canteens, an axe, and, at the bottom of the pile, two sleeping bags. Inside the sleeping bags were twenty-one four-pound bricks of what Clark recognized as high-grade cocaine.

He couldn't believe his eyes. He had never seen more than a pound of cocaine in his life. Its value was measured in ounces, and he was looking at a small mountain of it.

"It's cocaine," he said reverently. He and the trooper stared in awe at the heap of packages. They had hit a drug enforcement jackpot that most agents only dream of.

"I've got to call my office," Bill Clark said. "This is too big for me to handle."

"I've got to call my sergeant," said the trooper. "He'll sure as hell want to see this."

"I better call my wife," said Buck Slater, "and tell her not to wait supper."

It gets dark early in October, and it was pitch black when I arrived at Slater's garage. A sign in the door read: WE DO IT FAST OR WE DO IT RIGHT.

The office was dark, but a number of cars crowded the driveway. A few more people had come to join the party—a BCI man from Malone, another state trooper, and a senior DEA man, Newt Owens. He and I have worked together before.

Everybody looked at me when I walked in, but Newt waved me over and we shook hands.

"John T said you needed a fourth for bridge," I said.

"We do," Newt said. "Know where we can find one?"

He and I say dumb things like that to each other. I stepped back and looked around. The service bay had rear double doors, and these had been opened to throw a little light on the big Lincoln. The car stood there in the darkness, the trunk open, the camping gear spread out on the floor under a couple of work lights.

The atmosphere in the garage was tense. Everybody had agreed that the car had to be returned to the restaurant—it could be a vital link in a chain. And time was running out; any minute somebody could turn up at the Beef Palace, and not looking for a steak and fries.

I had walked in on the middle of the debate over what to do with the cocaine. It seemed logical to lock it away in the nearest safe place. But Newt Owens had another idea. He and his staff had put in a lot of time on this job, and he wanted to catch somebody, preferably Little Augie Vanvetti, in actual hands-on possession of it.

Newt is a little guy and he was surrounded by taller, meaner-looking officers, but he stood his ground. He did have the seniority; it was his decision and his neck. He wanted to leave the cocaine in the Lincoln.

"All of it?" asked the BCI man. "All eighty-four pounds?"

"Taking a big chance, ain't you?" asked a trooper.

"Just don't leave none of it here," said Buck Slater.

They compromised. Sixty-four pounds of the cocaine were dispatched to be locked up in the state police substation in Malone. About nine-thirty the big car was repacked and ready to go back to the Beef Palace parking lot. The problem was how to manage it. Buck's truck could tow the car but not push it.

Buck sidled up to Newt Owens. "I can start the car for you," he whispered, "iffen you tell those troopers to look the other way."

Newt clapped him on the shoulder. "Good man! Do it, and add something to your bill."

So Buck hotwired the Lincoln, and Bill Clark drove it back down the highway and parked it in the exact spot from which it had been taken. Nobody stepped out of the night to claim the car. Everybody took cover and waited.

Bill Clark went inside to give the night manager a very sketchy story about what was going on. Newt and I wound up in his car in a spot across the highway from which we had a clear view of the Lincoln, the starshine glinting on its chromework.

It was a crisp night, near to a frost. A mile away the lights of the little city threw a glow into the sky. I recalled that I had always wanted to come back to Ogdensburg and visit the Frederick Remington Museum again. But there was no chance this trip.

This was the first opportunity Newt and I had had to talk, but we sat there in silence for a few minutes. Then he stretched and yawned.

"What do you think happened, Hank? Wrong town or wrong day?" he asked me.

"I'll bet on the wrong town," I answered. "Somebody who didn't know upstate New York could easily confuse Ogdensburg and Hogansburg. They're only about fifty miles apart."

Newt nodded. "I'll buy that." He grinned. "I can see somebody sitting in Hogansburg right now, waiting for a big black Lincoln to show up." He looked at me. "You think maybe Augie's now holding hands with the Mohawks?"

I had been thinking about that. Hogansburg is on the Akwesasne reservation and Newt knew some of the Mohawks were friends of mine; his question was not as casual as it sounded.

"Not their style," I told him. Then I asked, "Why do you suppose Augie, or his car, is so far west? Didn't you say he always pushed his coke across the border at Rouses Point?"

"Right. Somebody screwed up, royally."

"Maybe he did plan to send the shipment across here at Ogdensburg or Hogansburg. Then he would have a straight shot down 401 to Toronto."

Newt shook his head. "Nope. His market's in Montreal. Augie's stuff always goes up 87 to the border."

I thought being so predictable would be a damn good reason for Augie to change his pattern, but I didn't say anything.

"How does he get the coke through Customs?" I asked.

"We know he uses ringers," Newt said. "He never makes a run across himself. He picks up some stooge and coaches him. Pays him well, too."

He grinned. "Last time we knew it was Vanvetti stuff he was using a man disguised as a Catholic priest."

"A father? How'd they nail him?"

"The inspector asked him a question about the stations of the cross. The guy didn't know the answer. He had two suitcases full of cocaine."

He yawned again. "On this deal maybe somebody got the wrong day. Maybe they were supposed to switch drivers tomorrow. But I can't figure why the first driver didn't stick around to see the car picked up by the next man. This is a lot of coke to leave in a parking lot."

I shook my head. "I figure the driver wouldn't know what was in the car. Augie would keep that a secret. The driver was just a driver, doing a driver's job."

"Whatever," Newt said. "Somebody screwed up." He closed his eyes and was asleep. I would wake him up in four hours. The restaurant was closed now; there were a few lights on where the night crew was cleaning up. The parking lot was dark, but I could see the black bulk of the Lincoln.

Eighty-four pounds of cocaine. That might not be much in the South Bronx or West Palm, but up here it was a huge amount. I looked at the Lincoln again. How many people were out searching for it? A car with that fortune in the trunk wouldn't be an orphan for long.

Yes, John T, this could be the drug bust of the year.

Two men in a Ford caught my eye even before they turned into the restaurant driveway. One man was excited, pointing at the Lincoln and talking to the driver. It was about nine A.M.; the morning rush had slowed down. The Ford pulled into the driveway, went past the Lincoln, drove around the take-out window, and parked. Both men got out.

One went over to the big car and walked around it. Maybe to see that all four wheels still had their tires, a big-city habit. The second man hurried to a pay phone at the far edge of the property, no doubt to call Little Augie. I thought if Augie had given his men portable phones as well as duplicate ignition keys he wouldn't have this mess on his hands.

The first man took out a key, fired up the Lincoln, and backed out carefully. He drove around the restaurant and turned left, heading north. The other man followed in the Ford. Several of us followed him.

It was a short trip. The Lincoln led us to a small motel on Route 11 outside Brushton. Of course, when we saw the big car and the Ford turn in, we had to drive on past and double back. Clark and the BCI man were somewhere behind us. Newt went into the motel office, and I sneaked around behind a hedge on the other side of an empty swimming pool.

The motel was two long one-story buildings facing each other across a wide concrete patio. The Lincoln stood at the far end, near a small group of people. Now I got my first look at the famous Little Augie Vanvetti.

He wasn't exactly little, more like a miniature giant. About five-feet four, he carried a massive build on rather short legs. He was well dressed in sports clothes and a hat with a feather in it. He had slick black hair and flashy rings on both hands.

Next to Augie were the two men who had driven up in the big car and the Ford. If there had been any cheering over the recovery of the Lincoln, it was over now. And nobody was paying any attention to the trunk.

A man and a woman stood with Augie in front of the car. They were both in their mid-thirties. Even from a distance I could see they were expensively dressed. The woman wore a tailored suit with a corsage pinned on her shoulder. The man wore a three-piece suit with a striped shirt, a maroon tie, and a silk pocket square. Augie was talking to them very earnestly. They were listening intently.

One of Augie's men came out of the motel room with some suitcases and stowed them in the back seat of the Lincoln. Expensive-looking luggage.

Newt joined me in the shrubbery. "So now we know where Little Augie is," he muttered. "He checked in late yesterday. The couple arrived the day before." He looked at the group by the car. "What's going on?"

"Looks like a rich uncle saying goodbye to a honeymoon couple," I answered.

Newt said, "You've got it. That's how Augie wants to get the stuff across."

We looked at each other. "Sure," I said. "Maybe we should throw rice when they leave."

Newt was frowning. "It might work," he growled. "It just might work."

There had never been any doubt that the cocaine was to be smuggled into Canada; the only question was how to bypass the Customs inspectors. The amateurs hide their stuff in a spare tire or in the bottom of a golf bag. The pros rearrange the upholstery or take out the radio speakers or put a false panel in a van or a truck. I have heard of fake oxygen bottles in an ambulance, and a double lid on a coffin.

Now, looking at the scene in the motel driveway, it was easy to see Augie's plan. The well-dressed man and woman, the expensive car, the new camping gear, a rich couple bound for a honeymoon in the wilds of Ontario—the last people on earth a Customs agent would suspect of handling contraband. The charade had cost him money, but Augie had a reputation to maintain. And he thought he had five million dollars' worth of cocaine in the trunk, for which he had a buyer waiting somewhere in Montreal.

"There they go," Newt said. I watched as the couple got into the Lincoln. Augie and his men stepped back as the big car turned and headed up the driveway.

Then, to our surprise, Augie took off. His Cadillac was parked by one of the rooms along with the Honda. Without a word Augie stepped over, got in, and drove up the driveway. When he passed us, I got a closer look at him: bull neck, shovel chin, arrogant expression.

Right, I thought. He's lost the Lincoln once, he's not about to let it out of his sight now.

"You drive," Newt said to me as we hurried out of the bushes. When we reached his car, he got busy on the phone. The question now was where would Augie's honeymooners try to cross the border into Canada? Our little parade was moving east on Route 11 about ten miles below the border. First was the Lincoln with the happy couple, then Augie in his Caddy, then Newt and I in his nondescript Dodge.

The sun was bright and the traffic was light, mostly logging trucks. This was the high plateau at the top of the state, north of the Adirondacks. Mentally I reviewed a map of the area.

The major traffic artery between upstate New York and Canada is I-87 at Champlain, to the east of where we were. There are five smaller and closer crossing stations. A smuggler had his choice; he might think he would get lost in the crowd at the bigger, busier crossing, or that the inspectors at the smaller stations would be less vigilant. Either way he would be wrong.

In twenty minutes we were in Malone. We expected the Lincoln to turn north, and it did. So Augie had changed his pattern; he would try something new.

"Will he take 37 and try to cross at Fort Covington or go 30 to Trout River?" Newt wondered.

"It'll be Trout River," I said. "Trust me. That will put him on a good highway straight to Montreal."

"Yeah, right," Newt growled. "If he gets across."

Where do you live? Where were you born? Where are you going? At the border the northbound traffic inspection is routinely handled by Canadian Customs, southbound by the U.S. inspectors. But at any time U.S. Customs can set up a northbound inspection lane and check the cars going into Canada. That's what they did at Trout River that morning.

Both agencies get a lot of anonymous tips. Maybe from jealous spouses, or business associates who feel cheated, or busybodies with mean streaks. Or, in our case, from another government agency.

Augie got to the border station at Trout River just in time to see the big Lincoln ahead of him pulled out of the inspection lane into a separate area nearby. All traffic was halted temporarily, and he watched as the agents had the suitcases taken out and opened and the trunk unloaded. A sniffer dog, a black Lab named Sherlock, was brought out. He went right to the sleeping bags, sniffed them both with great interest, and then sat down beside them. His handler rewarded him with one of his favorite toys.

The honeymoon couple stood by silently. Nobody had listened to them when they claimed they had just borrowed the car from a friend. Augie watched as they were arrested and led away and his car impounded. We were too far away to see the expression on his face.

Then Augie made what everybody thought was another mistake. He could have turned around and gone back to Florida. He could have told himself there was more cocaine where that came from. But when the inspector waved him through, Augie drove on into Canada, and as we learned later, he stayed there.

"He's gone," I said to Newt Owens. "Good riddance."

"Damn. That would have been a big arrest."

"Don't be a sore loser. Let's go pick up my car."

So Customs got twenty pounds of cocaine, a low-mileage Lincoln, and a bunch of new camping gear. As far as I was concerned, the job was over. All I had to do now was check out with John T and go home. I wanted to be on hand for pheasant season.

One of the troopers from the Malone substation had driven my car up, and it was waiting for me in Constable, a few miles south on Route 30. Before I headed home, I had a word with Bill Clark. I remembered that he was the only one who had actually seen the first driver of the Lincoln, the man Augie had entrusted the car to down in Lake George.

"What did this guy look like, Bill?"

"Big man," Clark said. "Fat. A smoker."

Now I knew Bill didn't work for me and he hadn't been home in a couple of days, but I asked him to do something else. I asked him to go back to Ogdensburg and check the hospital and the doctors' offices.

"Humor me, Bill," I said. "It's just a hunch."

When I got home, my phone was ringing. It was Clark. "Bingo," he said. "The big guy is in the hospital. Heart attack. Name of Edward Fulco, address in Newark. You want me to keep him covered?"

"Better ask Newt," I told him. "Thanks, Bill."

That would explain why Augie's driver had gone to the wrong town. He was sick, got confused, and wound up with a heart attack. Just before he blacked out, he shoved the Lincoln into that parking spot at the restaurant. Bill Clark said he collapsed right at the feet of a pair of off-duty firemen. Thanks to their training, they saw what was wrong, loaded the unconscious man into a van, and hustled him off to the hospital.

And that answered another question. Maybe there never was a second driver. Maybe this guy was supposed to drive straight to that motel outside Brushton to meet Augie and his honeymoon actors. Maybe somebody could ask him someday; right now I didn't care. I was tired, I had lost most of a night's sleep, and I had to call John T.

"Sure," I said, "Newt could have arrested Little Augie at that motel, but on what charge? Look at it this way, John T. Here's Augie standing in a public driveway by a car that Newt can't connect with him, and having an innocent conversation with some people about baseball or something.

"Newt was hoping Augie would at least get in the car, but he didn't. He didn't even put a fingerprint on it. And the object of the game was to bust Augie while he was holding, to establish criminal possession of a controlled substance, and so on.

"Anyway, you know what happened. Customs nailed the car and the coke, and Augie beat it into Canada. Be happy, John T. You've got the cocaine, it's not out on the street, and Augie's name will be mud down in Florida."

I thought that would be the last I heard of Little Augie Vanvetti. I was wrong.

Ten days later John T called me again. "How's everything up there in the boonies?" he asked. I don't like that "boonies" talk. Yes, we are in the mountains with trees and fields and rivers. But we are not backward. Downstate they have dope dealers in the schoolyards, and the streets aren't safe at night. Up here we have clean air and a utility that burns old auto tires to make electricity. So who's ahead of whom?

"Fine," I answered him. "How's everything in smog city?" I waited. I knew he wanted something. He began by bringing me up to date on the Vanvetti family.

The newspapers had reported the seizure by Customs of twenty pounds of high-grade cocaine, and the

DEA made sure the news got down to West Palm. The Vanvetti family was understandably upset. Little Augie had been entrusted with eighty-four pounds of cocaine, and now only twenty pounds rested in a government vault.

Thus Augie had allowed sixty-four pounds of valuable merchandise to disappear. Then he himself had vanished into Canada without announcing any plans for a vacation. The family felt this was the act of a heinous and disloyal double-crosser. The Vanvettis wished to settle accounts.

"Here's the deal, Hank. Little Augie is hiding up in Montreal, and he wants to come home."

"Well, maybe his mother will be glad to see him."

"No, he doesn't want to go down to West Palm. He knows there's a contract out on him down there. He wants to come here. If we give him protection, he'll tell us some family secrets."

"Way to go, John T," I said. "Thanks for calling."

"Wait a minute, Hank! We want you to escort Augie back across the border. Just bring him to Plattsburgh. It's your back yard, you can do it easy."

For these little odd jobs John T carries me on his time sheet as a consultant. The extra money does come in handy. I stalled for awhile, but I agreed to do it.

Two nights later I was standing under a tree somewhere very near the border. I could have thrown a rock into Canada if I had known which direction to throw it. It was very dark and very cold, and it was beginning to snow.

Once again I was a part of one of John T's little schemes. Little Augie was afraid to show himself in public. He knew or suspected the family was having him watched. John T and the various agencies involved had arranged that Augie would cross the border secretly on foot.

On foot. People do it almost every day. Or night. At the border down in Texas are miles of chain link fence. Up here there's no fence, just miles of woods. Heavy, thick woods with trails and paths that run north and south.

Most of the illegal aliens from Europe and the Near East try to enter the United States this way. A contact in Canada puts them in touch with a guide who brings them down close to the border, at night of course. The guide tells them to "follow this path a hundred yards and you'll come to an open place and a blue sedan. The driver will take you to Glens Falls or Albany or wherever."

The helpful guide collects his fee and departs, forgetting to mention the motion detectors and the heat-sensitive devices the U.S. Border Patrol maintains in these woods. Several hundred illegals try to walk across every month. Several hundred get caught.

More snowflakes touched my face. It was late October but not too early for the first snow of the season. When I had left home to drive up to Champlain, the barometer was falling and the sky was full of leaden clouds. Snow clouds.

At the office complex outside Rouses Point I checked in at the Border Patrol office and met the rest of the reception committee. Newt Owens was on assignment somewhere, and Bill Clark had gone back to his home office. There was a DEA agent, a state trooper, and a Border Patrol officer who was our host. We drank coffee until it was time to load into a couple of Patrol vehicles and drive to this spot.

"Augie will be wearing a red-and-black hunting jacket and a fur hat," John T had promised me. "You can't miss him." An agent in Canada was to start Augie on the path that would lead him to where we waited. And of course the Border Patrol had agreed not to demonstrate their electronic surveillance devices to our guest.

Someone to my right snapped on a flashlight, probably to check the time, and turned it off again but not before I saw more snowflakes. Someone else shifted his feet in some dry leaves. My legs were beginning to ache from the cold. I wondered if Augie's family gossip would be worth all this bother. I wondered if I had enough firewood for the winter. I wondered ...

There was a flicker of light somewhere ahead. The Border Patrol officer walked forward in the darkness. "He's coming," someone muttered and snapped on a lantern. I strained my eyes to see, and then I could make out a form coming through the trees. As he came into the light, we saw a short, heavyset man wearing a bushy fur hat and a red-and-black jacket. He held out his hand.

"Hi, fellows. I'm Augie Vanvetti."

I stood rooted to the ground as the others moved forward. Then I turned and ran back the way we had come as fast as I could. I wanted a telephone and right away.

The man with the chunky build in the red-and-black jacket was not Little Augie. He was another ringer.

The Canadian police found Little Augie sitting on a bar stool at Montreal's Mirabel Airport. He had a first-class ticket to Paris in his pocket, and would have been halfway there if the snow squall hadn't socked in the airport and canceled all flights.

Since I was the closest person who knew Augie by sight, I was driven up to police headquarters in Montreal to make a positive identification. The Canadian authorities decided to hold Augie for awhile; they had questions of their own about his narcotics distribution network.

Augie was very bitter about the whole thing. Setting up the stand-in was supposed to buy him enough time to get out of the country. But his look-alike was spotted right away, and by a retired hick cop. And then the weather; nobody had predicted that it would snow.

The DEA charged Augie's ringer with obstructing justice—they couldn't charge him with impersonating a criminal—but they finally let him go.

So I lost another night's sleep. I was bushed when I got home, but I still had chores to do.

And John T called. "So it wasn't the bust of the year," he said, "but don't worry about it. We'll have plenty of other chances, old buddy."

"Sure we will," I said, "but next time, don't call us, we'll call you."

The Land
Healers

A very pretty young woman opened the door to
Rory's office and gave him a brilliant smile. "Got
a minute?" she asked.

Rory frowned at the interruption; his desk was over-
loaded. But he said, "Sure, April. Come on in."

The girl was tall and slender, with deep blue eyes
and jet black hair cropped short in a youth's haircut.
She wore the uniform of the newly formed Mohawk
police force. There was no sidearm on her wide leather
belt, but a large utility pouch was slung over one hip.

"Thanks, chief," she said. "Davie's got something to
show you."

A boy of about fourteen had followed her into the
office. He had a Mohawk's dark features and stocky
build. He was holding a coffee can with both hands. He
crossed the room, placed the can on the desk, and
stepped back.

Rory leaned forward and peered into the can. It was
empty except for a large hypodermic syringe. The syringe was crusted with dirt, and the inside of the barrel
was coated with a dark brown stain that could have been

blood. The needle looked very bright and very sharp. Rory looked up at the boy. "You didn't touch this, did you, Davie?"

"No, sir. I used two sticks to pick it up."

"That was smart. Where did you find it?"

"By the creek on my grandfather's place. My dog was chasing a rabbit."

Rory looked at the syringe again. Hospitals and doctors with very sick patients used large needles like this. Where did this one come from?

"Did you tell anybody about this, Davie?"

"No, sir. Only April. I showed it to her, and she said we should bring it to you."

Rory glanced at the girl and nodded. "Good thinking."

She gave him another smile. April Summers was fresh out of college and a probationary member of the force. She had a charming manner, and the visitors to the reservation loved her despite the occasional traffic tickets she handed out.

"Tell Mr. Horn what else you found, Davie," she said.

"I saw two more of these," said the boy, "and some other stuff. Bandages and things. April said you ought to know because you're in charge of the environment."

"Not exactly," Rory said. "I help clean up the pollution." The sign on his office door read:

ST. REGIS MOHAWK TRIBE
Environmental Studies
Rory Horn, Director

Years ago big industries near Massena in upstate New York had disposed of manufacturing waste by dumping it into a nearby river, the Raquette. The waste contained PCB and other noxious chemicals that contaminated the rivers and soil on the Akwesasne reservation. After thirty years the pollution had reached alarming, even life-threatening, levels. Now, after thousands of water and soil samples had been analyzed and hundreds of committee meetings had been held, the cleanup was finally under way. Rory's job was to coordinate the effort between the manufacturers, the EPA in Washington, and the DEC in Albany.

Now here in the coffee can on his desk was a new form of pollution—used hypodermic syringes—and it wouldn't wait for a committee.

April and Davie were looking at him expectantly. "Saddle up, chief," April urged. "We've got tracks to make."

Rory pushed aside the files on his desk and stood up. He locked the can in a cabinet and looked at Davie. "You'd better show me where you found this thing."

Rory's jeep was parked at the side of the Mohawk Community Building. He held the door open while April folded herself into the back seat.

"Thanks, chief."

"Don't call me chief," Rory said. "Douglas Solomon is a chief. Noble Frankland and Mike Lean are chiefs. I'm not a chief."

She grinned at him impishly. "Yes, sir. Sorry, sir."

Davie hopped in beside Rory. The August sun was beginning to bake the pavement as Rory drove down Hogansburg's Main Street. Midmorning traffic was light; later in the day tourists would come to buy souvenirs and tax-free gasoline and tobacco.

Many of the Mohawk men were employed off the reservation as high-steel workers, raising the skyline of Manhattan still higher. A number of women worked at the Tru-Stitch shoe factories in Malone and Bombay.

Rory drove past the shops and the big casinos and turned left onto Cook Road. This paralleled the course of the St. Regis River as it and the Raquette flowed through the reservation and into the St. Lawrence, the international waterway.

Rory had majored in environmental science; he had graduated the same year the federal Superfund Cleanup Bill was passed. Since then he had seen small animals die, birds drop out of the air, fish become unfit to eat, all because of the PCB contamination.

Now cleanup efforts had begun, but they had to be controlled. Fishing and hunting and a whole way of life had to be restored, not destroyed.

He was driving past empty fields dozing in the summer heat. To the left a line of trees marked the path of the river. Eagles once nested in those trees, and their feathers were still used in tribal ceremonies.

Along the river were burial sites that must be protected. Under the trees grew flagroot, a plant used for medicinal purposes, and the aromatic sweet grass that was highly prized by the women in weaving their intricate baskets. Rory couldn't let those things fall prey to hungry bulldozers.

Davie pointed and Rory slowed the jeep. Tire tracks angled away from the road to follow a high bank above a stream. "Down there," Davie said.

Rory stopped and they got out. A glance at a survey map told him this was Turtle Creek. Now, in summer, the stream was dry, the bank steep and overgrown. From the edge of the bank they could see the stream bed. It was choked with weeds and alders that almost concealed two fifty-gallon drums. Broken weeds showed the path the drums had made as they rolled down the bank.

"April, follow those tracks," Rory ordered. "Davie, you stay put."

He slid down the bank, the heels of his half boots digging into the dried mud. The cover of one drum had come off; the tightly packed contents had spilled out on the ground. Rory saw more syringes, blood-soaked dressings, scalpels, empty and half-empty vials. He prodded the mass with a stick and uncovered a torn warning label that read *Infectious Material.*

He felt a surge of anger at whoever had so little regard for human life as to dump dangerous and possibly lethal material where someone could stumble into it. Thank God the stream is dry, he thought, or this stuff could have been spread for miles.

April came down to stand beside him, a serious look on her young face. "Hospital waste, right?"

"Right," Rory growled.

April made a disgusted sound. "Think what might have happened if Davie had stepped on one of those needles. Or another kid had started playing with them. What kind of person would do this?"

Rory shook his head. They climbed back up the bank where Davie was waiting for them.

"You find anything?" Rory asked April.

"Four more drums farther down. Any idea where this came from?"

Rory nodded. "All the printing on those drums has been spray-painted to hide it, but I did make out the letters MA."

"Massachusetts," offered Davie.

"Right. Maybe one of the hospitals in Boston." Rory put his hand on the boy's arm. "Listen, Davie, we've got to keep this quiet until we clean it up, all right?"

"You got it, Mr. Horn."

"What do we do next, chief?" April asked.

"Don't call me chief," Rory said absently, and then he looked at her in surprise. "We? I thought you were on traffic detail."

She turned to face him. "I want in on this, Mr. Horn. I know I'm just a rookie, but I want to help nail someone for this. Can you get me assigned to your office?"

Rory hesitated and then nodded. This girl didn't have much experience, but she did have determination. And he could use some help. "All right. I'll get back to town and call the DEC in Syracuse to get a disposal team up here." He moved toward his jeep. "And I'll call Mark Benjamin; he's BCI."

April knew that was the NYS Bureau of Criminal Investigation. Rory handed her his radio.

"Call your sergeant and do what you have to do to seal off this area."

"Right." April was looking down at the stream bed and its odious burden. "Who could do something like this?" she burst out suddenly. She turned to Rory. "I can't be impersonal about this! This is more than just a crime! It's, it's..."

He touched her arm. "I know what you mean." She was feeling the same sense of outrage he had experienced many times. Softly he said, "Our great-grandfathers believed that any defilement is an injury to the land. And the land must be healed."

April nodded. "I remember," she murmured, "because the land is mother to us all." For a moment they stood in silence, watching the heat waves shimmering on the horizon. Then she gave him a brilliant smile. "Let's go to work, chief."

"Don't call me chief," Rory said as he stepped into his jeep. "Come on, Davie, we've got things to do."

On the way back to town Rory drove by the site of one of the test wells. "There's a sensor down there that monitors the ground water," he explained to Davie. "That way we'll know if the pollution gets any worse, and we can do something about it."

"Suppose the water does get real dirty?"

"We can pump it out and clean it."

All the remedial work should be that simple, Rory thought. We can remove contaminated soil or water and clean it or replace it, but that takes time, lots of time. Maybe someday there'll be a shortcut. He knew work was in progress to find a chemical way to neutralize the toxic effects of PCB.

"Until we get it licked, we've got to keep the pollution from getting any worse."

"I read you, Mr. Horn," Davie said.

Twenty-four hours later the stream bed had been hygienically cleaned. Men in plastic suits had collected all the drums and loaded them into a large trailer. They had shoveled up the spilled waste and a considerable amount of the dirt around it. Everything would be transported to an incinerater near Rochester.

April had met the disposal team at the south border of the reservation and escorted them to the site without attracting attention. Everyone worked quickly, remembering the near panic that had resulted when hypodermic needles washed up on public beaches a few years before.

Mark Benjamin had driven up from his office in Syracuse. He had been a friend of Rory's father, and he was still Uncle Mark to Rory and his family. Dressed in a dapper three-piece suit in spite of the heat, Mark looked like a successful real estate salesman. But some residents of Attica and Dannemora had learned that beneath the silver hair and friendly smile was a lawman with the tenacity of a bulldog.

Rory and Mark stood on the bank and watched as the men secured the last of their gear. April climbed the bank to join them. Mark watched her approach with an appreciative eye for her trim figure.

Rory made the introductions. "Mark Benjamin, meet Officer April May Summers."

The name caught Mark by surprise. "You're kidding!"

"No, he's not," April said. Ever since high school her name had spawned innumerable jokes.

"That's my real name," she said grimly.

Quickly Mark held out his hand. "Glad to know you, officer."

"April will be watching this for me," Rory explained. "I've got a top-level meeting with some Washington brass two days from now."

Mark nodded and looked at April appraisingly. She bristled under his gaze. "You think I'm too young for the job, Mr. Benjamin?"

Mark shook his head. "No, not too young," he said with a grin. "Maybe too pretty."

In spite of herself April blushed.

"Now then, Officer Summers," Mark said briskly, "how do you see the problem?"

April frowned, concentrating on her answer. "These drums we found are fiberboard, not steel. They're not heavy. The hospital waste is all lightweight material. That says one man can handle a loaded drum. He can drop it out of a truck and roll it anywhere. Down a bank like this, for instance."

Mark nodded in agreement, and April went on. "We found two drums here and two drums at each of the two other spots. Two drums at a time says a small van or a panel truck. To me that adds up to one trip at a time by one man in one vehicle."

Mark nodded again. "That's the way I read it." Rory saw the sudden smile on April's face. "Just two suggestions," Mark said. "This person may be using more than one dump site here on the reservation. You might check out some other likely spots."

"Being done now," April said.

"And tell your Warrior leaders what's going on. They can be a big help in watching for a vehicle with any of the New England plates. There may be another load in the pipeline now."

"Already done," April said. The Warriors were the militant arm of the Mohawks; their mission was to protect the sovereignty of the Mohawk nation.

They walked back to the road where Rory's jeep was parked. "We found enough scraps of labels to know this stuff came from hospitals in the Boston area," Mark said.

He turned to face April. "We've seen this kind of thing before. The hospital thinks it's dealing with a legitimate disposal service. The front man has all sorts of credentials. But once the refuse is picked up, the gang takes this kind of action." He gestured at the ditch behind them.

"And dumps it where some child could get into it."

Mark noted the anger in April's voice. "Don't worry," he said. "We'll get whoever's responsible."

Rory had a question. "Remember last year when you caught those people dumping asbestos on the Onondaga reservation? Why do people think they can take advantage of Indians like this?"

"Don't get riled, son," Mark said. "Reservations are still open territory. This bum thinks he's found an ideal place to dump illegally." Mark turned to April. "And that was his first mistake, right, Officer Summers?"

She smiled grimly. "Right, Mr. Benjamin. If he comes back we'll be ready for him."

Rory dropped Mark in the parking lot of the Bear's Den Restaurant and went on to his office. There was a message for him to call Chief Douglas Solomon.

"Will we be ready for the senator and his party day after tomorrow?" the chief asked.

Rory was tempted to ask for a delay, but it was out of the question. There were still decisions to be made about the cleanup work, and he had to speak for the tribe.

"Yes, chief, we'll be ready." Rory called his wife and said he wouldn't be home for dinner.

April's voice on the phone was excited. "I've got a pickup with a camper top and Mass plates out here on Cook Road. Could be our boy!"

It was ten-thirty. The meeting with the party from Washington was at eleven. "You handle it," Rory said. "Get Jake to help you."

"No time," April said. "Jake's over on Cornwall Island. This guy is headed for the same spot by Turtle Creek. When he sees we've worked it over, he'll turn around and split. I'll hold him as long as I can, but come arunnin', chief!"

The line went dead. "Damn!" Rory slammed the phone down. His door opened and Chief Solomon walked in, looking as always like an investment banker.

"Don't worry, Rory," the chief said, "I'll handle the delegation until you get back. Go on and take care of that scum."

Rory stared at him in amazement. "How did you know?"

"April called me first. She knew you might hesitate. That's a smart gal. Now go."

Rory found April crouched behind the hood of a police car and pointing a shotgun at a little man standing in front of a small camper. The car was swung across the road, blocking the truck's passage. The man in front of the camper was very well dressed, and he seemed very relieved to see Rory.

"How do you do, sir," said the little man, smiling. Rory noticed he was not sweating even though he was wearing a jacket. "I'm glad you're here. I'm afraid there's a little misunderstanding with this young lady. She won't let me pass, and I am in a bit of a hurry."

The little man seemed completely at ease. Rory wondered if April had made a mistake. But the man's accent was pure New England. Let the girl play out her hand, he decided.

"I'm Charles Wakefield, at your service, sir," the man continued smoothly. He offered Rory a card which Rory made no move to accept. "Custom hair styling. Best little shop on Boston's East Side, if I do say so."

"Hi, chief," April greeted him from behind the car. "Would you please go and look inside that rig?" There was a tremor in her voice, but her grip on the gun was steady.

Rory walked over to the rear of the pickup.

"Sir, you can't do that," the little man said primly. "That would constitute a search, and you have to have a warrant for that."

"You're on an Indian reservation here, Charlie," April said to him, "and we make our own rules."

Rory smothered a grin as he opened the back of the camper. Inside were two familiar fiberboard drums. He looked back at April and held up two fingers.

"Oh, I see," the little man said pleasantly. "You think I might have been planning to discard those containers. I was just doing a favor for a friend." He shrugged elaborately. "He said it would be all right to drop them off. Or maybe I got the wrong road."

He moved toward the door of his truck, but April raised the barrel of her shotgun. He stood quite still.

In a very surprised tone he said, "Oh, I understand. That would have been a misdemeanor, wouldn't it?" He smiled at April and Rory. "Well, just let me pay a fine, and I'll be on my way." His hand dipped into his pocket and came out with two fifty-dollar bills showing between his fingers.

He edged closer to Rory and extended his hand. "Let me settle up for the trouble I may have caused. Here, you and the little lady have a good time for yourselves."

Rory shook his head. He saw that Charles Wakefield was beginning to perspire.

"Let's have one of those drums out here," April said, "and see what Charlie has been carrying around."

Rory eased one of the drums down to the pavement. The lid was secured by a metal strap. He opened it and lifted the lid. The drum was packed with hospital waste, needles, sponges, bandages, bloody refuse. He tilted the drum so April could see the contents, then replaced the lid.

April shook her head. "Charlie, you should know that stuff is dangerous." She paused and the little man looked beseechingly at Rory. "Who sent you up here, Charlie?" April asked.

There was the sound of a car on the road behind them. A jeep with two men in it coasted to a stop beside Rory's vehicle. Both men were Mohawks, both wore army camouflage uniforms, both carried weapons. They were Warriors; the larger man was Jake Hightower, one of the Warrior leaders.

They walked forward and stood beside April. Jake looked at the shotgun, and April handed it to him quickly. Jake turnd to Rory and said, "Solomon got me on the radio." He looked at the little man dispassionately. "Who's this?"

"This is Charlie," April said. "He's been dumping hospital waste." To the little man she said, "Once more, Charlie, who sent you up here?"

The man wiped his forehead. "You can't arrest me! It isn't even my truck!"

April shook her head. "You disappoint me, Charlie." She stepped out from behind the cruiser and walked over to the drum of waste. She wrenched off the top and held it in front of her as she looked at the contents. Then she slammed the lid shut and walked back slowly, holding something in her hand.

"Take off your jacket," she said to Charlie.

"I won't!" His voice was a squeak.

"Help him, Jake."

The two Warriors moved to either side of Charlie and helped him out of his jacket. Jake's big hands remained on his arms, holding him in a viselike grip.

April stepped closer to the man and slowly raised her hand. She was holding a large hypodermic syringe, its barrel filled with a red liquid. She held it upright in front of his face. He watched, fascinated, as she pressed the plunger and a drop of red appeared at the tip of the needle.

"What, what is that?" he squeaked.

"You ought to know, Charlie, you brought it up here. Now let's try that question again. Who are you working for?"

He shook his head, sweat running into his collar. "You can't do this!"

April shook her head. "Have it your way, Charlie." The needle glinted in the sunlight as she brought the syringe closer and closer. Charlie strained against the hands that held him.

Rory was alarmed. He had been amused by April's performance, but now maybe she was going too far. He took a step closer, ready to interfere.

April was only two inches taller than the man, but she seemed to tower over him. She lowered the syringe to his forearm, the needle an inch away from his skin. In a soft voice she said, "My great-grandfather would call this getting shot with your own arrow."

"All right!" Charlie said suddenly. "All right! This isn't worth a C-note!" He looked from Jake to Rory frantically. "I'll tell you the deal, but get this chick away from me. She's crazy, you know that?

"This guy calls me about twice a month. I meet him at the Liberty Bar and Grill. He tells me where to make the pickup, and he gives me a hundred for each run. Sometimes an extra twenty as a bonus."

He talked for several minutes. Finally Rory said, "That's enough. Take him and hand him over to the state police down on Route 37."

The two Warriors escorted Charlie Wakefield to their jeep.

Then Jake Hightower turned and walked back to Rory and April. He picked up April's shotgun and frowned at her. "You're on probation, Summers. You know you're not supposed to carry firearms," he said sternly.

"I know, Jake," April said. "It's my brother's. I just borrowed it. Please don't tell the sergeant."

Jake said nothing but handed the gun to Rory. He pointed at the syringe that April had dropped on the hood of the car. "You want to tell me about that?"

April picked it up. "Oh, this?" She pressed the plunger and emptied the red liquid into the palm of her hand. "It's Kool-Aid," she said. "Cherry flavor."

"And you had the needle in your bag," Jake said. "I thought so." Rory saw the ghost of a smile on his face as he turned to leave.

"Hold on a minute, Jake," Rory said. "What April did was illegal, you know. It was entrapment or intimidation or something. The police will never be able to hold him."

"Yeah, maybe," Jake said slowly. "But look at it this way—we used the sparrow to catch the hawk. Right?"

"Right," April said eagerly.

"Right," said Rory slowly.

Jake put his hand on April's shoulder. "Not bad, rookie," he said.

"Thanks, Jake."

They watched the two Warriors drive away with their prisoner. Rory looked at his watch. It was after twelve. He looked at April. "What did you need me for? I didn't do anything."

April turned away from him. "How did I know Jake would get here?" she asked in a very small voice. "And I knew you would back me up, no matter what." Her voice broke, and Rory looked at her in surprise. He saw her eyes were filling with tears.

"I was afraid. I've never done anything like that." Her lips were quivering and her hands shaking. Rory reached out and put his arms around her and held her until the tears and the trembling subsided.

Much later that afternoon Rory and Mark Benjamin sat over cups of coffee in the Bear's Den. "It was a clean sweep," Mark was saying. "Everybody connected with that hospital waste dumping is behind bars."

He paused and looked out the window. A tourist family was having its picture taken with a tall, very pretty young woman in a Mohawk police uniform.

"How was your meeting?" Mark asked Rory.

"We're getting there," Rory said. "The parts per million levels are still a big issue. But by the time we're through, we'll have a clean environment."

April appeared in the doorway. She looked around and then walked over to their booth.

"Nice work, officer," Mark said gravely.

"Thank you, Mr. Benjamin," April said. She looked at Rory. "I'm afraid I came unglued there at the end," she said ruefully.

Rory shook his head. "Forget it."

"Look, April May," Mark said gently. "You and Rory are both doing the same job, protecting your land. That's worth getting uptight about."

She gave him a grateful smile. "Thanks." To Rory she said, "Well, I guess that makes us partners, doesn't it, chief?"

"Yes, it does," said Rory, "Only don't call me...oh, never mind."

Murray and Mister Smart Nose

"He just got lucky," Murray said.

"You'd have to take that car apart to find that stuff where I hid it."

"No, Murray, he's had special training."

"Training, spaining! He got lucky again, I tell you!"

"It's progress, Murray," I said as soothingly as I could. "It's new technology."

"This is technology? Four feet and a cold nose is technology? Give me a break, Irving!"

I deliberately changed the subject. "Anna wants you to retire, Murray. Why put it off? Go to Florida. Take a condo."

"And live next door to that idiot son-in-law of mine?"

"You don't have to live in West Palm, Murray. I hear Lauderdale is nice."

"I wouldn't live in the same state as that bum."

I shut up. There was no use talking to him when he was in that frame of mind. And especially now that his pride had been hurt. A dog named Bingo was ruining his business.

Murray and I were connected with the smuggling trade. He hid things, such as packages of narcotics or currency, and I changed things, such as the identification numbers on stolen cars.

We operated near one of the busiest borders in the country, the border between the United States and Canada at the top of New York. Up there the smuggling never stops; just ask the Border Patrol in Champlain or Rouses Point.

Murray had a machine shop next door to my garage and used car lot. That made it nice because strange cars could come and go without attracting local attention. We were on Route Nine less than two hours below the border. You might say we had a ringside seat.

The illegal traffic is heavy. Cocaine comes north from Florida on its way to Canada. Heroin comes into Canada from places like Ghana and moves south into the States. Firearms, all kinds, move both ways. A big volume item is tobacco. It goes into Canada by the ton because most of the cigarettes exported from Canada are smuggled right back in.

And people, illegal aliens from Europe and the Far East trying to evade our Immigration and Naturalization Service. And cash, millions of dollars of it. Annually? Try monthly.

Anyway, let's say you've got a few pounds of cocaine you want to take to market in Canada without interference from Canadian Customs. You could do what the amateurs do and hide the stuff in your spare tire, or shove it in the bottom of a golf bag, or sew it up in a stuffed elephant.

Or you could go to Murray. He was a concealment specialist, known to be an expert at hiding small packages in automobiles that were to be driven past customs inspectors. Wherever he put your merchandise, in a false door in the trunk, in the back of the seat, in place of the speakers, every joint, every seam would look like the factory original.

"There's no respect for workmanship any more," Murray griped. "What's the world coming to?"

That was the problem. Murray's work was picture perfect, but now appearances weren't enough. Canadian Customs had brought in a sniffer dog, a dog trained to locate marijuana and cocaine by smell. Bingo looked like a black Lab, but actually he was a Belgian shepherd, very intelligent and with the keenest nose in dogdom. (In case you didn't know it, we've got sniffer dogs on our side, too.)

"This is man's best friend?" Murray snapped. "His fleas should have fleas already."

Bingo's educated sense of smell let the inspectors see through plastic or paneling or upholstery. One sniff and Murray's work was rendered null and void. "By a dog yet," Murray groaned. "The shame of it!"

How do you sympathize with someone who is a fossil, a has-been? "Retire, Murray," I would say.

"What are you, my father now?" he would say. He was stubborn; he wouldn't give up.

"I'm not finished with you yet, Mister Smart Nose!"

A man from New Jersey gave Murray his next opportunity. He had six "bricks" he wanted to transport into Canada, secretly, of course. He was in a hurry and kept looking over his shoulder.

Murray worked quickly. He found an old ice chest and put a false bottom in it with the packages underneath. Then he put in about five pounds of fish and some water but no ice.

By the time the car reached the border the chest and the trunk would reek of ripe fish. Murray threw in a rod and a reel and saw the man on his way.

I had a contact on the other side of the border who told me what happened. The overripe fish did not sidetrack Bingo. Canadian Customs impounded the car and the cocaine and the man from New Jersey.

Another round to Bingo.

Murray was despondent, but a few days later he had another turn at bat. A man appeared in his shop with a small case full of cocaine and a pocketful of cash. He had a Florida tan and a young lady by his side.

Murray had an inspiration. He told the man to trade his car in on a camper that happened to be on my used car lot, and to come back in two days to pick it up.

"Now, Mister Smart Nose, we will see what we will see."

The next day I went into Murray's shop with a news flash. "Listen, Murray," I said, "the Mounties are taking Bingo on a demonstration tour next Thursday. He'll be part of a program to teach school kids about drugs. Send this guy and his coke across the border on Thursday, and you'll have nothing to worry about."

Murray's eyes lit up. "Right! We sneak by when Mister Smart Nose isn't looking!" Then he frowned. "No, Irv. Then I'll never know who can outsmart who, will I? Nope, I'll be ready for him on Wednesday."

So when the man from Florida came back with his girlfriend to pick up his camper, I gave him his title and then listened in while Murray was briefing them.

"You're man and wife," Murray said. "You're going camping near Toronto. Hang up your clothes in the closets, and put your toothbrushes in the bathroom. Buy yourself some milk and fruit for the icebox. Understand?"

The couple nodded. We went inside, and Murray moved to the tiny kitchen area. He opened a cupboard door and pointed at the shelves. They held a few cans of soup and vegetables. Murray tapped on the back wall. "I put a new panel here," he said to the man, "Your property is behind it."

Then Murray pointed at a small bag of flour and a rack of spices. "Now listen good. Before you get to the border, you pull over in a rest area and stop. You spill the flour and the spices all over the floor. Understand?"

The couple nodded again. "Don't worry; things get spilled in campers like this all the time."

Then Murray took a small bottle out of the spice rack. "Now, you be sure to open this bottle and pour it on the floor in front of this cupboard door."

He opened the bottle and held it under their noses. It was oil of peppermint; the pungent smell quickly filled the camper. Murray capped the bottle again. "This is to fool Mister Smart Nose," he said to me.

"So now," he said to the man with the Florida tan, "tomorrow's Wednesday. You stay in Plattsburgh tonight and cross at Champlain in the morning." He pointed at the flour and the spices. "Can you handle everything?"

The man grinned. "Piece of cake." He took out a roll of bills and paid Murray his fee. Then the couple got in the camper and drove away.

"It's beautiful," I said. "Murray, you're a regular Cecil DeMille. You should get an Academy Award." I knew how hard he had worked; I wanted to make him feel good.

Murray smiled. "Now we'll see what's what."

Wednesday morning we waited, Murray in his little shop and me in my garage. I figured the man with the Florida tan should hit Champlain about midmorning. It was a pretty day, and I knew traffic at the border would be heavy both ways. I didn't think the man and his girlfriend would do anything to attract attention to themselves, but border inspectors are smart. In an eight-hour shift they can see as many as four thousand cars. They develop certain instincts about people and their reactions to questions.

"Anything yet, Irv?" It was Murray at my door.

"Not yet, Murray. Go back to your own place."

I was worried about him. The stubborn old fool was about to give himself a heart attack over what he thought of as a personal problem. And he wouldn't listen to me.

Like I said, I had a contact on the Canadian side. I had described the camper to him, and I was waiting for his call. I got it just before noon. The camper went through.

I walked over to Murray's shop. He saw me coming and had the door open, so nervous he couldn't stand still.

"The camper got past customs," I told him. "There was a line of cars, and they had to wait. Then one of the agents came and asked them the usual questions and stuck his head inside the camper and looked around. Then they waited some more, and then the inspectors waved them on through."

"Good!" Murray was delighted. "Was Mister Smart Nose there?"

"Yes, he was there. His handler took him in the camper for a few minutes, but they came right back out." Murray was nodding and grinning.

"So the guy from Florida is on his way to Montreal with his coke," I said. "You happy now?"

Murray rubbed his hands together. "Yes, Irv, I am. So I finally fooled Mister Smart Nose."

He looked around his little shop and sighed. "You know, Irv, you may be right. It is time to quit. I think I'll try Daytona."

And he did. Two days later Murray and his wife Anna had their car packed and the house in the hands of a realtor.

"Goodbye, Irv. Come see us."

"Goodbye, Murray. Stay healthy."

I knew he'd be happy down there. I'd miss him, but his kind of talent was obsolete now. Not just because of dogs like Bingo. There's a lot of high tech like sonic imaging and magnetic X-rays for detecting stuff these days. Murray would always be a real craftsman; maybe he would build himself a boat down there in Florida.

There's no reason he should ever know what really happened that Wednesday morning at the border.

Yes, Bingo did smell out the cocaine in spite of the peppermint and the bay leaf and the oregano. But the agents decided to leave it where it was and let the camper go on through. They had a good reason.

The setup in the camper was just too elaborate, too professional. It suggested to the inspectors that the contraband hidden in the trailer must be very valuable stuff. Also that the man driving the camper might have some very interesting business associates somewhere in Canada. People the police would like to meet.

So they let the camper drive on, and a plainclothes detail picked it up and followed it, all the way to a house in a suburban area of Montreal. And a day or two later the police hauled in a big narcotics distribution ring.

But I didn't lie to Murray. The camper did go through just as I said it did. Later on I told Murray that I heard the man with the Florida tan was in jail.

"Good," Murray said. "He should grow old and have bad teeth."

Then he told me the man had paid him with counterfeit one hundred dollar bills.

Your Law,
Our Land

Rory Horn hugged the trunk of the birch tree and wished he could make himself invisible. The top branches were still swaying from his rapid climb; if either of the two men looking for him glanced up, he would be seen.

And probably shot. Rory was certain he had just seen a load of illegal firearms being smuggled into Canada. He was also sure any witnesses would be extremely unwelcome.

The men on the ground below were both white, both armed with Israeli-made Uzi weapons, both dressed in brown uniforms. They followed the faint trail to the river's edge, searching the low underbrush, watching for a boat on the water. They retraced their steps and paused under the clump of birch and pine.

"Where'd the bastard go?"

"Damn Indians. Always snoopin' around."

"You think he saw anything?"

"Nah. I spotted him as soon as he showed up. He split when I yelled out."

"We can't take chances. You go that way and meet me back at the truck. And put the gun away; remember we're on an Indian reservation."

With a sigh of relief Rory watched the two men disappear through the brush. He remembered the meeting that afternoon in Chief Harry Blackwell's office.

"Firearms are funneling through the New York side of the reservation into Canada, and we don't know how the shipments are being made." The speaker was grim-faced as he looked around the table.

"How do you know the arms are going through our territory?" asked Chief Blackwell.

"Our intelligence gives us that much, but that's all we've got."

"This contraband, what exactly is it?"

"Big ticket items. Assault rifles. Grenades. Anti-tank missiles, probably surplus from the Gulf." The speaker was Art Bowers, field agent of the Bureau of Alcohol, Tobacco and Firearms.

This meeting was supposed to be about fishing violations in the St. Lawrence. Rory was there to give a status report on the pollution cleanup operation by the EPA and the New York DEC. Non-natives were encroaching on Mohawk fishing areas. The Akwesasne Mohawk police didn't have the manpower to enforce the laws; the tribal council had to appeal for cooperation from the Canadian authorities.

At the table was a uniformed sergeant of the Royal Canadian Mounted Police, another from the Ontario Provincial Police, a man in plainclothes from the Sûreté du Quebec. Bowers of the ATF and Farley of the FBI had turned up at the last minute, and Chief Blackwell had permitted them to sit in.

Art Bowers had asked to speak. He was in his late thirties with glasses and thinning hair and the beginning of a paunch. To Rory he looked more like an accountant than a field agent.

"The word we get is that the Warriors are stockpiling a lot of armament," Bowers said, "as if they didn't have enough firepower already."

Chief Blackwell interrupted. "We don't need that kind of gossip," he said sharply. "If you get any proof of that, Mr. Bowers, you bring it to me."

Art Bowers shrugged and sat down. Rory saw the look he gave Farley, a look that said "dumb Indians." It was the superior attitude of some white men, and Rory resented it.

John Farley said, "We've been stopping every truck and trailer and camper that comes on the reservation. But so far no luck."

"It's been bad for business," Chief Blackwell said, "but we haven't objected."

"Sorry, chief," Farley said. "I hope none of your people are involved in this, Chief Blackwell. You've had enough on your plate these past few months."

Rory knew what he meant. There had been internal clashes in the tribe between pro-and anti-gambling factions. There had been gunfire, deaths. The papers called it the "gambling wars" and labeled the Warriors militant hotheads. The tribe didn't need any more negative publicity. The meeting went on; the Canadian representatives promised cooperation.

When the men were out of sight, Rory slid down the tree to the ground. He had the classic Mohawk profile, the strong nose, the heavy chin. He wore his black hair long, caught at the back of his neck with a short blue ribbon. While it was common to see Indian men with blue eyes, Rory's eyes were a light brown.

He did not follow the path but worked his way along the river bank. It was late spring, and a horde of black flies followed him. This was Cornwall Island, the largest island in the St. Lawrence, the river that marked the boundary between the U.S. and Canada. The river flowed through the center of the Mohawk reservation near Massena, New York. The Akwesasne Indians were on the state side, the St. Regis on the Canadian side. A community of Indian families lived on the island with their schools and churches, but there were stretches of undeveloped land that were isolated and empty.

Rory had left his truck parked near a trailer that served as a field headquarters for the DEC and EPA engineers engaged in taking soil and water samples. Rory had majored in environmental science; now he represented the tribe in the pollution cleanup studies.

"Every truck, every trailer, every camper," John Farley had said. Rory had followed a hunch that afternoon after the meeting, and blind luck had paid off. Now he knew how the contraband firearms were being handled. But before he could tell anyone, he had to get off the island.

Up ahead he heard a car engine start. Lying prone on a slight rise, he parted strands of high grass and peered through them. The two vehicles he had seen earlier were moving out. The men had given up their search for him. Rory rose and began trotting toward the area where his Ranger was parked.

He wondered whom he should tell about what he had seen. There were many law enforcement agencies involved. There was nothing new about smuggling along the U.S./Canadian border. It could be cigarettes, narcotics, firearms, even illegal aliens from Europe. Most of it was concentrated farther east in the Swanton sector at the Champlain border crossing.

There the agents had to contend with a heavily traveled interstate that ran from Albany to Montreal. And there was the Amtrak railroad, and even the boat traffic on Lake Champlain. All saw their share of smuggling activity.

Rory decided to tell Uncle Mark what he had seen. Mark Benjamin had been a friend of his father's. He was a senior agent with the New York State Bureau of Criminal Investigation. His office was in Syracuse.

He would tell Mark, and Mark could tell whomever he chose. Mark knew that any publicity linking Mohawks with anything illegal would be especially bad now. Legislation favorable to the Mohawks was pending in the statehouse down in Albany. Bad publicity could kill it.

It was late when Rory headed his little pickup over the bridge from the island and started for Hogansburg. In the western sky he could see the lofty St. Lawrence International Bridge. Lights were beginning to twinkle along the length of the span that linked the two countries.

It was full dark when he drove up Memorial Street to St. Regis Road and headed for Main Street. He passed a shop with a big sign that read WELCOME TO AKWESASNE—LAND WHERE THE PARTRIDGE DRUMS.

There was little traffic. Here and there at intersections he saw the dark blue state police cars parked with their lights off. The troopers and the Canadian provincial police had maintained a presence on the reservation since the armed conflicts months ago. The Warriors resented it deeply as an insult and an intrusion.

Light spilled from Billy's Bingo Hall, but most of Main Street was deserted, the big casinos standing dark and silent, their employees out of work and restless.

Rory stopped at the Bear's Den, a complex of stores, a restaurant, and a service station. A few late tourists were there, filling up with tax-free gasoline and buying tax-free cigarettes.

"I'm looking for Jake Hightower," Rory told one of the attendants. He mentioned his name and turned away. Jake would get the message. The Warriors had an excellent communication network, and Jake was one of the leaders. And a friend of Rory's despite the fact that Rory did not believe in violence and had never joined the Warriors.

But there were hundreds of men like Jake, determined to preserve the sovereignty of the Indian nation against all intruders. They were militant and well armed.

Each Warrior was to possess a 12-gauge shotgun with forty rounds or a .223 rifle with one hundred rounds. Handguns were optional. "The Warriors will at all times be a defensive force," read the guidelines. "We will never initiate any action unless so directed by the War Chief. Our responsibility is to protect the people of our nation and our Mother Earth and the things that dwell upon her."

"What do you call yourselves?" Rory had asked Jake once. "Militia? Minutemen?"

"We're the peacekeepers," Jake growled.

Outside of Hogansburg, Highway 37 was dark. Rory had the radio tuned to CKON, the reservation station. He was listening to a rock number when a car materialized on his left. He waited for it to pass, but it slowed to match his own speed. Rory was vaguely aware of a dim shape in an open window, and then a blast of flame and noise. Lightning seared into his shoulder and across his head. The after-image of the flash lingered for an instant and then faded. The world went black, and the little truck nosed across the shoulder of the road and came to a gentle stop in the ditch.

The erratic behavior of the headlights caught the attention of a state trooper car coming up 37 from the opposite direction. The cruiser saw the little pickup canted over in the ditch, turned sharply, and braked behind it.

From a great distance Rory heard voices.

"Looks like another drunken Indian."

"Can it, George. He's not drunk. He's been shot. Hold that flashlight steady. Hey! I know this guy!"

Someone was shaking him gently and calling his name. Rory opened his eyes and thought he saw the face of an old friend.

"Nash?" he asked weakly. "Is that you, Nash?"

"It's me," said Nash Seymour. "Don't talk, old buddy. We'll get you out of here."

Rory came back to consciousness in a bed in the hospital in Massena. He saw a pleased grin spread across the face of the trooper standing by his bedside.

"You'll be all right, Rory," said Nash. "Just take it easy." He and Rory had gone to high school together in Salmon River. It was pure chance that Nash and his partner had been patroling on Highway 37 when someone fired a buckshot charge at Rory. And pure chance that Rory had not been killed. Some instinct had prompted him to throw up his left arm defensively. A slug had creased his scalp, another had torn through the muscle of his upper arm. He would wear bandages and a sling for some time.

Another person by the bed grasped his hand. Rory blinked and saw Uncle Mark smiling down at him. "You're all right, son," Mark said. "The doctor says no concussion." Mark Benjamin looked like a successful insurance salesman. He always wore an old-fashioned three-piece suit with a chain across the vest. With his iron gray hair, he could have been forty-five or sixty.

"Donna?" Rory asked in a faint voice.

"She's fine. I told her there had been an accident. She wanted to come, but I told her I would bring you home as soon as the doctors got through with you."

"Thanks. How did you..."

"I heard it on the radio, on the police band." Mark glanced behind him. "Captain Barnes is here. Feel up to some questions, son?"

Rory nodded. "Something to tell you, Uncle Mark," he whispered.

"Later, son."

Captain Barnes was a bluff, hearty mountain of a man in the full uniform of a captain of Troop B. He wasn't disappointed that Rory could tell him nothing factual. Rory hadn't seen the gunman, didn't know the make of the car, knew no reason for the attack. "We'll talk again tomorrow, son," Barnes told him.

From the hall Rory heard Barnes's voice, stern and authoritative, addressing the troopers and the hospital staff. "I want this kept absolutely quiet, you understand? I don't want things stirred up on the reservation, you hear me? We don't want last summer all over again. If it gets out that an Indian was shot, the Warriors will have barricades up by morning. I won't have it, you hear?"

He stuck his head in the door. "Mark, if the boy comes up with anything, you let me know chop-chop."

"You got it, captain."

Barnes disappeared. Nash and his partner were gone. The doctor took a last look at the big white bandage on Rory's head, felt his pulse, and told him to go home and to bed.

Mark said, "I know you've got one hell of a headache, son, but you were lucky. A dozen stitches, no broken bones." He held out his hands to help Rory stand up. "Let's go home. There's someone outside waiting to see you."

Rory leaned on Mark for support. His dizziness and nausea cleared somewhat by the time they reached the parking lot.

Waiting beside Mark's car was Rory's friend, Jake Hightower. He was a bit taller, more heavily muscled than Rory, a fierce man with a permanent scowl on his face. Without a word he grasped Rory's hand. "Someone will pay for this, Rorhare Horn," he said, almost formally.

Then Jake straightened and looked at Mark. "As I told you, I've got a team watching Rory's house." He indicated the tiny radio at his belt. "The boys tell me a man has arrived there. He's white, armed, hiding by the garage." He paused. "I read it as somebody planning a surprise."

Mark nodded. He didn't seem alarmed. If Jake Hightower had his Warriors on the scene, the scene was secured. "Jake, suppose we plan a little surprise of our own?"

"What say?" Rory asked drowsily.

"Never mind, son."

Rory lived off the reservation near the small town of Helena. Home was a modified trailer, surrounded by flowerbeds and shrubs and a wading pool in the rear. Behind the garage was an old barn that housed Rory Junior's pony, Major. The house was dark except for a light in the kitchen where Donna sat waiting for her husband.

A car turned into the drive from the highway and stopped. Out stepped a tall man with his arm in a sling and his head swathed in white bandages. A shorter, older man crawled out from behind the wheel, and together they walked up the path toward the back door. It was late, there was no moon, but faint starshine glimmered on the tall man's white headdress.

A man emerged from the side of the garage. He stooped and brought a rifle up to his shoulder. He took careful aim at the man with the bandage on his head. The night was quiet, a soft breeze touched the leaves of an oak tree by the path. The man tracked his target carefully.

Then a strong hand reached out and seized the barrel of the rifle, twisted it upward, wrenched it out of the man's grasp. Other hands seized the man. "What the hell..." he gasped before a gag was placed in his mouth. He struggled, but many hands silently bore him away.

The two men paused by the back door. "All right, Jake," a tiny voice spoke through a radio. "We got him."

Jake Hightower began unwinding the bandage from around his head. "Anybody we know?"

"Nope. Outside talent."

"Okay. Take him into the barn and tell Sam to do his thing."

The smaller man walked back to the car and helped Rory extricate himself from the back seat; it was difficult with one arm in a sling. "Damn it, Uncle Mark! I don't like hiding behind someone else."

"Save it, young fellow. I'm calling the play here. Jake was glad to be the decoy. You could have got yourself shot all over again."

"Or Jake could have."

Mark shook his head. "No way. Jake's boys had the intruder spotted as soon as he came on the place. He never would have gotten off a round."

"Then, damn it, why did you want Jake to be the decoy?" Mark grinned. "Why take chances? Come on and let's see if Donna has any coffee made."

The gunman, who had never been north of the race-track at Saratoga, nor out of sight of neon or concrete, was terrified. What was to be a simple two-hundred-dollar hit on a lousy shirttail Indian had gone terribly wrong. His guns were gone, he had been picked up and handled like a baby, he didn't know where he was, he didn't know who the silent, purposeful men surrounding him were, or what was going to happen to him. Whatever it was must be bad. Very bad.

He felt a post at his back; he was standing, his arms pulled back and bound. He faced ahead in darkness blacker than any he had ever known. From somewhere came the sound of a drum, faint, then stronger, insistent, rough, primitive. And then there was a light, a circle of bright light, shining on a rough wooden door. The drum became louder. The door opened.

A horrible figure appeared. A swarthy face with garish streaks of yellow and orange slashed across the cheeks, lips parted in a terrible grin. An Indian, a goblin of childhood, a nightmare returned.

The figure wore a leather vest-like garment, his dark arms and shoulders bare and gleaming with oil or sweat. In beaded headdress with a circle of upright feathers, leather chaps on his legs worked with red and black symbols, his feet stamping in time with the drum, the figure advanced slowly toward him.

From his belt he drew a long wicked-looking knife and tested its edge on his thumb, his eyes never leaving those of the trembling white man. He reached out to touch the white man's cheek, and the man screamed and shrank against his bonds.

The ghostly Indian danced, keeping his eyes on the white man's face. He made slicing motions against his fingers with the knife, nodding and smiling, twisting the knifeblade in the beam of light.

A quiet voice spoke in the white man's ear. "Who sent you here tonight?"

"I'll tell you! Just keep him away from me!"

Mark and Jake sat on one side of the kitchen table, Rory and Donna on the other. Donna was a non-native, a white girl Rory had met in college and married after graduation. Donna couldn't keep her hands away from her husband. She held his arm, constantly touched the bandage on his head, asked him over and over how he felt.

Rory tried to reassure her. "It looks worse than it is," he told her. "The orderly had to take off a lot of hair." He still felt lightheaded. He looked for Rory Junior, then remembered that Donna had sent him to sleep over at his grandmother's house.

Jake was listening to his little radio. "Your visitor is on his way to town, Rory," he said quietly with a nod to Mark. "He'll be our guest for awhile."

Donna looked at the window. "I thought I heard a drum out there," she said in a puzzled tone. "Did anyone else?"

"It was just a tape," Jake said. "Martha uses it in her exercise classes."

Mark handed Rory a small capsule. "Take this, son. I asked the doc for it. It will clear your head for a few minutes while we do some talking. Then Donna can tuck you into bed."

"All right," Donna said sternly, "but just for a few minutes." She put her arm around Rory protectively. "This Indian needs his rest."

The medicine helped; Rory's headache abated, and he felt almost normal. He squeezed Donna's hand and leaned forward. "Here's what I know, Uncle Mark."

Jake started to rise from the table. "No, stay here, Jake," Rory said quickly. "This concerns the Warriors as much as anybody."

He looked at Uncle Mark. "Art Bowers says firearms are getting through the reservation into Canada. He implied that the Warriors might be involved. I want to show him how wrong he is."

"So do I," said Jake in a low tone.

"The FBI and the ATF are checking every truck and trailer that come on the reservation, and they come up empty. But there's one vehicle they don't bother with. One vehicle that's on the reservation almost every day, in and out of Canada every day."

Mark and Jake were listening intently. Rory was tempted to prolong the suspense, but a twinge of pain banished the thought. He looked from Mark to Jake.

"UPS," he said. "A United Parcel Service delivery van. Either a real one that's been stolen, or a damn good duplicate. UPS delivers everything from baby clothes to generators, and nobody gives it a second thought. It's as innocent as an ice cream truck in August."

Mark slapped the top of the table. "Damn!" he said softly. "Damn!"

Jake nodded his head slowly, his eyes shining.

Quickly Rory related how he had seen two UPS trucks parked side by side in a deserted field on the island. One truck wore Canadian plates, the other New

York tags. The drivers were transferring heavy wooden crates from one to the other.

"There must have been a third man there," Rory mused. "Someone who got a good look at me, someone who tried to have me ambushed on the way home."

"Right," said Uncle Mark. "And someone who very soon will think you are dead, that the hit man finished the job tonight."

Rory stared at him in astonishment.

"Look," Mark said. "These people found out you were in the hospital the same way I did, by monitoring the police frequency. That's when they decided to send someone else out here, the man Jake's team collared.

"I'm going to have Nash Seymour phony up a report on his radio about you cashing in out here tonight." He looked at Donna. "Sorry to be so blunt, girl. It has to be done."

Donna's face was white, but she nodded. "I'm all right. I just wish it were over."

Mark turned to Rory and Jake. "Once that's done, I'll set up something with Barnes and Farley. I'll use a phone I know is secure."

"Wait a minute," Rory mumbled. "There's something else." He was fighting to keep his eyes open. A soft lassitude was spreading over him. But he couldn't close his eyes, not until he'd said something that was important.

"Bowers suggested that the Warriors had something to do with this smuggling. We know that's not true, but it's not enough that we know." Rory closed his eyes, shook his head, and opened them again. "Other people have to know it, too."

He raised one finger and tried to point it at Mark. "Right now..." his voice was a whisper; he tried again.

"Right now the Mohawks might get a seat in the assembly down in Albany. That could be important to us."

"Maybe," growled Jake. "Maybe not."

Rory stared at him. "Better'n nothing," he mumbled. "Le's don' argue about it now." He concentrated on pointing his wavering finger at Jake.

"All right, old buddy. You're the peacekeepers. So keep some peace around here."

Then Rory was fast asleep, snoring gently.

Jake looked at Mark. "What did he mean by that?"

"I think I know. Here's what we'll do..."

The little radio clicked softly. "He's coming down Hilltop Drive," a voice said, "passing First Street."

"I copy," Mark Benjamin replied. "Heads up, everybody. We'll take him at Third."

He looked across the seat at Rory and grinned. "Here we go, kid." Rory felt better after a day's rest. He grinned back and held up both thumbs.

In the back seat of the car Chief Blackwell leaned forward, a wide smile on his face. "Go for it!"

Beside him Art Bowers, agent of the Alcohol, Tobacco and Firearms Bureau, frowned. "I still think we need more people."

No one answered him.

Rory had protested strenuously. "We don't need Bowers. He's got an attitude problem."

"Yes, we do," Mark ruled. "The game is called intra-agency politics. Trust me."

Rory had wanted this to be an all-Indian affair. But he couldn't shut out Uncle Mark. And that opened the door to other white men. What the hell, he thought, I can live with it as long as the Mohawks get some of the credit.

It was a bright spring morning on Akwesasne. Children were in school. Housewives coped with laundry or shopping. A man astride a Wheelhorse riding mower appeared and began cutting grass near the corner. Mark's car was parked on Cherry just off Third; they had a clear view of the intersection. Down the street a tow truck backed out of the equipment garage and turned left on Third; it moved past the corner and stopped.

The chocolate-brown UPS van coming down the street was a familiar sight in this or any other residential neighborhood. The driver, neat in his brown uniform, sat perched on his stool behind the windshield. He always stopped at stop signs, obeyed all speed regulations.

The driver halted at the intersection, waited, and then blew his horn impatiently at the tow truck blocking his way. Shaking his head in frustration, the truck driver got out and raised the hood.

The man on the riding mower rode over to the curb to watch, enjoying the driver's predicament. Unnoticed, a station wagon ghosted to a stop close behind the UPS van. Two men got out and quietly approached on foot.

The van driver decided to try to drive around the stalled truck, but found his way blocked. A station wagon was behind him, the riding mower was now out in the street to his left, and on his right two men stood at the open door of the van. They were pointing guns at him.

"What the hell..." He looked ahead and saw a man aiming a rifle at him across the hood of the truck. The yardman was kneeling behind his mower and pointing a gun at him. The men all had very grim expressions.

The van driver had the good sense not to reach down for the ignition key. He left the engine running and raised his hands above his head. All four men converged on the van. They were Indians, each with a tiny radio at his belt and a red-and-yellow band on his left arm. Other cars arrived, and the group grew into a small crowd.

Art Bowers ran up and began issuing orders. "Put the prisoner in that car... read him his rights...don't touch those crates...keep this traffic moving." A reporter who had received an anonymous invitation to be in the vicinity this morning appeared. He plied Bowers with questions.

"Is it true the Warriors made a citizens' arrest?"

"Well, yes..."

"Can I get a picture of you and the Mohawks to-gether?"

"Well, yes..."

To the delight of the bystanders and the reporter, one of the wooden crates from the cargo section of the van was opened. Labeled "Hydraulic Pump Repair Parts," the crate contained M-60 machine guns liberally coated with grease.

A state trooper sought out Rory and Mark, who were standing at the rear of the crowd. "They made a clean sweep down in Westchester this morning, Mr. Benjamin," he said. "Nailed the whole outfit."

"Glad to hear it," said Mark. "The Ontario police did a good job, too."

The trooper hesitated, looking from the older white man to the younger Indian man. "How come the Warriors got to make the bust, Mr. Benjamin?" he asked. "We could have done it."

"Sure you could, son. You're the professionals. But this is Mohawk territory. Rory, you explain it."

Rory didn't make the usual comments about sover-eignty and self-rule and jurisdiction. He just said, "It's your law, but it's our land."

The trooper nodded slowly. "Right."

Jake Hightower, who had been the man on the riding mower, walked up. "Everything go to suit you, Mr. Benjamin?" he asked.

Mark punched him on the arm and grinned. "Couldn't have done better myself."

Jake looked at Rory. He pointed at the red-and-yellow band on his arm. "We've got one of these for you any time you want it, Rory."

"Thanks, Jake. I'll think about it." Rory had to go to his office, but he was reluctant to leave. The street was filling with people, and the atmosphere was almost that of a block party.

A television crew from Plattsburgh had arrived and was filming everyone and everything in sight. Jake and his Warriors had discreetly put their weapons out of sight and were mingling with the crowd. The other tribal chiefs were on hand with Harry Blackwell, smiling and shaking hands.

Mark Benjamin was ready to leave. "This won't hurt a bit down in Albany," he said to Rory. "Your nation may get that assembly seat some day." Rory nodded. "My best to Donna."

Rory watched Uncle Mark drive away. He turned to go but stopped when someone called his name. It was Art Bowers.

The agent walked up, his face flushed with excitement. "Ah, Horn," he said, "you Indians did a fine job this morning, a mighty fine job." The patronizing tone set Rory's teeth on edge, but he realized Bowers was being sincere. What the hell, Rory thought, some white men can't help being clay-headed.

"Thanks, Bowers," Rory said. "Be our guest any time."

So Long, Lana Turner

"This is not a simple car theft," I declared. "I think you may have a major crime on your hands here, officer."

"Let's hope not, sir," the young trooper said politely.

"Well, you just wait and see if you don't." I knew I sounded peevish, but I couldn't help it. First I'd had to walk almost two miles out of my way to call the troopers, and then wait almost an hour, and then when one shows up he looks like just a rookie.

I pointed at my evidence. "It's not just the New Jersey license plates up here in northern New York. It's the man's empty wallet. It's the safe deposit box key that was hidden. And the facial tissue with lipstick on it. Or maybe that's blood. All that looks mighty suspicious to me!"

"Yes, sir," he said, still very polite. "And you found these things over there in the high grass?" He made it sound like only a senile old man would go poking around in tall grass and weeds.

"I told you. I pick up empty cans." I shook my plastic bag of empties. "And bottles, too."

"Yes, sir. What makes you think these items are connected with each other?"

"Because they weren't here yesterday afternoon," I said triumphantly.

We were standing on the side of a road about two miles north of where I live in Clinton County, New York. It's a simple two-lane road that runs between the village of Ausable Forks and the larger town of Keeseville. There's a little turnout there, just a place to pull off the highway to stretch your legs or switch drivers or change a baby's diaper. It's small, only big enough for three cars at a time, surfaced with gravel and outlined with big stones. No picnic tables, and only one trash bin that hasn't been emptied for a year.

The turnout doesn't offer much in the way of scenery, but you can see the Adirondack Mountains to the south, and if you climbed a tree, you could see Vermont across Lake Champlain to the east. It was June but a nice breeze kept the black flies away.

"The sun was shining on an empty beer can," I explained again, "and that led me to find these things. I thought it was peculiar that they should all be here at the same time, so I walked down to Tim's Esso and called your dispatcher. That's a mile more than I usually walk." I didn't mean to sound so surly, it was just that I was excited. I'm a widower; I live with a married daughter and I build bird houses. Life is pretty dull, but now out of pure luck I was about to be involved in a police investigation.

"I'm sorry about that, sir," the young trooper said. "You could have waited for me at the service station."

"Oh, that's all right." I could tell he was sincere. "I'll cut back some tomorrow."

After I made the call, I walked back to the turnout to wait. I was sitting on a big rock when the New York State Police car pulled up, a dark blue sedan with a broad gold band on the sides and the state seal on the doors. The officer who got out was very young. I don't know why I had expected someone more my own age.

His name tag read MARION, S. He was tall and lanky, and I had to admit he seemed competent enough. He was wearing the new state police sidearm, the Glock 9mm semi-automatic pistol I had read about it the paper.

Right away I had to be entered in his notebook.

"Your name, sir?"

"Hank Foster."

"Is that H-e-n-r-y?"

"I prefer H-a-n-k."

"You happened to be walking by when you found some items you thought were suspicious?"

"No, I did it on purpose. I mean, I walk for my health."

"And you're retired, sir?"

I wanted to rattle my bag of empties at him and say I was in the salvage business, but didn't. I admitted I was retired.

I put the things I had found on the hood of the trooper car. The wallet was the conventional type that goes in a hip pocket with slots for credit cards and so on. This one was good leather, not plastic, and it was curved and flattened to indicate that it had been carried in a pocket for quite a while. Still, it was not worn or scuffed, not ready to be discarded. No initials on the outside, no identification on the inside.

Officer Marion, S. picked it up. "Maybe some tourist just bought himself a new wallet and stopped here for a break and decided to transfer his stuff from his old one to the new one." He didn't sound like he really thought that was what had happened, and I didn't either.

"No, I don't think so," I said. "He wouldn't forget his key." I held it up to make my point.

Someone had cleaned out the wallet before he threw it away, but he missed one thing. I almost missed it myself. Jammed down in one end, behind the flap where large bills go, was a flat safe deposit box key. You couldn't see it and you would never know it was there unless you happened to feel it with your fingers. No bank name, just three stamped numerals that must be the number of the box.

Marion, S. put the key in a small envelope and picked up one of the license plates. They were this year's issue, in perfect condition, not defaced in any way.

"You'll want to contact the New Jersey Department of Motor Vehicles," I began, "to find out who these plates were registered to." Marion, S. gave me the same look I used to give a student who had said something quite obvious. I shut up and we looked at the plates in silence.

I guessed he had the same questions in mind as I had. Why stop out here on the highway and take the plates off a car and throw them away? Answer: because someone is looking for that particular car. But why then attract attention by driving around in a car with no license plates on it? Answer: you wouldn't. You would have another set of plates ready to put on the car. Did the same person who owned the car also own the now-empty wallet? I didn't have an answer for that.

The young trooper was walking around the turnout, looking at a few old tracks in the gravel and the white painted stones that needed painting again. I stood by the trooper car and kept quiet.

He came back and picked up the New Jersey plates again. "You know, Mr. Foster," he said carefully, "there's a lot of cars that cross the border up at Champlain. Both ways. And not all tourists, if you know what I mean."

"I know," I said, but I hadn't thought of it before. Of course he meant all the smuggling that goes on in and out of Canada. Champlain isn't two hours away from this spot. There are ten border crossings in New York and Vermont, and Champlain probably is by far the busiest. Customs and the Border Patrol have their hands full. Smugglers use pleasure boats on the lake and the Amtrak train, but the favorite means is the private car. The biggest volume is in cocaine.

"I'll put the word about these plates on the computer, but chances are the car these belonged to is long gone. Up in Quebec or down in West Palm." He glanced around the turnout again. "As for the rest of it, Mr. Foster, I think it's just coincidence."

I couldn't say anything to that. If there had been a crime, a murder perhaps, and if it was connected to cocaine smuggling, Officer Marion, S. couldn't discuss it with me. I was a civilian, and to him a pushy one at that. But I was sure of one thing: whatever was going on, I wanted to be in on it.

I tried to sound sheepish, which is not easy for me to do. "I guess you're right, officer." I paused for a moment to change the subject. "Can I ask you something?"

"Shoot."

"What's the 'S' for? Steve or Sam?"

"Steve."

"When you find out about those plates, will you let me know, Steve, please? I'll be here tomorrow."

He grinned at me. "Sure thing, Hank."

He picked up my trophies and drove away. I picked up my bag of empties and started home. I was jubilant. This had been a big event for me and it wasn't over yet; I still had my foot in the door.

A car passed me on the way to Keeseville. The driver was Lana Turner. I caught a glimpse of her bright blonde hair and her cheerful smile. I waved and she waved back.

Lana Turner isn't her real name. She's a young woman who reminds me of the sweater girl queen of my undergraduate days. About six weeks ago a car stopped alongside me on the highway and the driver leaned out to ask me a question. She was a young woman with great natural beauty—blue eyes, cute chin, a generous mouth. Her hair was brass blonde, and she wore a tight yellow sweater. I gave her the name Lana Turner.

She asked me where the Page place was, and I told her. She thanked me and smiled before she drove away. It was the special smile pretty young women can give to older men. It's warm and open and unguarded because they don't have to be wary of being misunderstood or thought flirtatious. It's a very rare smile, and one that a lonely old man will treasure.

I was dog-tired when I got home; those extra two miles hadn't been in the energy budget.

That night I went to sleep thinking about the empty wallet. What became of the credit cards and the baby pictures and the other trivia that must have been in it? Why would anybody stand on a highway in plain sight and clean out another man's wallet? Answer: he was looking for something and he was in a hurry to find it. What was so important? Answer: not cash. He would have found that right away and heaved the wallet with everything else inside it. It had to be something small, like a claim check, or a receipt. Or the hidden key he didn't find.

So what did happen to the contents, the bits and pieces of someone's identity? Answer: they were still there, somewhere around the turnout. Why was I so sure? Whoever had taken the wallet in the first place had been careless. First, he didn't find the key. Then he didn't dispose of the wallet very well; anybody could have found it. So he would have been careless about the little, unimportant things. And I would find them.

If I was lucky, I would have something else to show Trooper Steve Marion this afternoon. He would be glad to have me helping him on this case. I picked up my plastic bag and started down the road. I am doing all this walking to avoid an operation I don't want to have, by the way. Last fall my seventy-year-old heart staged a mutiny. An angiogram showed that the left side was not working right; an artery was silted up or something. A cardiac specialist young enough to be my grandson told my daughter and me there was nothing to be too alarmed about; he did bypass surgery all the time and almost always successfully.

The bypass job didn't sound good. First they saw through the middle of your rib cage and make an opening large enough to hide a football. Then they root around and find the diseased artery and chop it out. Then they splice in a vein they have pirated from one of your legs. I said no. We negotiated, my daughter and the doctor on one side, me on the other. I won a six-month postponement during which I promised to eat sensibly, go to Sunday school, and exercise moderately.

That's what I'm doing. I walk about three miles every day. Of course I can't repair the damage to that one artery, but I can make the others work harder. The doctor says I'm still a prime candidate for a heart attack, but I do feel better.

That's how this stretch of road became an extension of my front yard. I know every crack and bump, every weed and tree. The empty cans and bottles began to bother me. At first I picked them up and threw them farther back in the bush. Then I began to save them. If I am going to spend so much time on this road, by thunder it is going to be clean.

Now I carry a bag for the empties. A local charity redeems them, and the money from the deposits goes to a children's hospital. There is a tiny sense of accomplishment, and I don't care what the natives think. They're as bad about littering as the tourists. Worse, because they live here.

On my exercise route I pass the Page place. This is a large garage set back from the road. A sign over the door reads PAGE AUTO REPAIR. Several cars are always parked in front and by the side of the building. A large field in the rear is crowded with other cars, new and old, kept, I assumed, to provide repair parts.

Farther back is the Page residence, a one-story frame house. A small house trailer is parked on one side. There is a scraggly flower bed with a concrete bird bath. The house needs paint, the yard needs raking.

There always seemed to be activity around the garage. I knew Walter Page by sight, and if I saw him as I walked by, I would wave and he would wave or nod in return. He was a heavyset man with a ragged black beard. His son, Walt Junior, was one of those unfortunate kids whose life was already over.

He had been a football star in high school and had his picture in the paper twice. After graduation he could at least have gone into one of the armed services, but he didn't. Now he worked in the family garage and would never see the outside of Clinton County. The boy who had been so fast on his feet now walked with a flat-footed step and was getting heavy like his father.

Where Lana Turner fit into this family I didn't know. She must have been kin from somewhere, come for a long stay or maybe permanently. After she arrived a few weeks ago, the Pages brought in the secondhand trailer that was parked beside the house. I assumed that was her living space.

Lana must have done the shopping for the household; I saw her every day or so driving back and forth into town. I felt sorry for her. She was too pretty to be stuck up here in the mountains. If she stayed, she would wind up like so many other young girls: too short on youth, too few choices, fated to marry a man who worked with his hands instead of his head.

"Pretty young woman," I wanted to say to her, "don't waste your life here. Don't let the world leave you; catch up while there's still time." I never spoke to her, of course. It was just an old man's thought as he trudged his endless miles. But I would wave and she would wave back and smile at me.

At the turnout I was lucky. The trash bin was the obvious place to start searching and in twenty minutes I had found three credit cards and a driver's license, all issued in the same name. They were in the bottom of the bin, the credit cards bent double and the license ripped in two. Digging for them was a filthy job, but I didn't mind. I was paying my dues in the detective business.

These things had to be from the wallet I found yesterday. Someone had stood right here and gutted the wallet, probably dropping them on the ground. Then he picked them up and rammed them down the side of the trash bin as far as he could reach. That might have seemed safe enough, but it was a careless way to try to hide a person's identification.

I sat down on the big rock to examine my discoveries. The credit cards didn't tell me much; the license was the jackpot. It was a buff-colored New York license issued to a Thomas Swinney with a post office box address in Syracuse, New York. His height was five-ten, his eyes brown, his age thirty-eight. The photo was too tiny to show much except a jowly face with thin black hair and a mustache. He could have been anything from a bartender to a truck driver.

I was delighted. I couldn't wait to introduce Mr. Thomas Swinney to my friend Steve Marion, the trooper. Even if this wide spot in a back road had been the end of the line for him.

When Steve arrived, I stood up. "Howdy, Mr. Foster," he said. I had hoped he might say something like "Howdy, partner."

"Those license plates were from a stolen car, all right."

"Yes," I said, trying to keep the excitement out of my voice, "and this may just be the man who stole it."

Steve was impressed with my finds. He didn't waste any time; he got on the radio in his car and asked for any available information. He wasn't being polite now; he was all business.

I sat on my rock and waited. I was sure we were on the track of some criminal activity. This area has a history riddled with crime. The road I walked on every day had seen its share of criminals. During Prohibition it was one of the roads bootleggers used to transport whisky from Canada down to Albany and on south to New York City. Big touring cars, loaded so heavily their springs were flat, crept down it at night to hide in barns during the day while the cargoes were split up into other cars and driven south.

Illegal liquor was big business then, but it couldn't hold a candle to the smuggling today. Illegal aliens get the most newspaper coverage. "Sixteen foreign nationals discovered in false floor of truck." They come from half the countries of the world to try their luck with the Border Patrol. Cigarette smuggling goes on constantly, but the customs agents can usually spot the contraband from fifty paces away.

The biggest game of all these days is narcotics smuggling. The wave of cocaine has swept north from Florida and reached into Canada. It travels north across the border by courier, and payment in the form of cash comes down, again by courier. Like cash, cocaine is small in bulk, easily concealed, worth more than its weight in gold.

Interstate 87 is our main north-south artery, since it runs from Albany to Montreal, four lanes all the way. But, as in Prohibition days, it is more discreet to use side roads for moving a load of coke or cash. And, as in the old days, the one place strange cars can go in and out unnoticed is the friendly neighborhood auto repair shop. Quite suddenly I thought of the Page place, just a mile away.

"Thomas Swinney's got a record. Grand theft auto." I jumped at Steve's voice behind me. "Sorry, Hank," he said. "I didn't mean to startle you."

"That's all right," I said quickly. "So he's got a record? And I suppose you found out he's missing?"

Steve was puzzled. "How'd you know that? Yes, his P.O. says he doesn't know where Swinney is."

"His P.O.?"

"His parole officer. Says Swinney hasn't reported in the last month or so."

"Well, he's not missing. He's up here. We've just got to find his body."

Steve gave me a long look. I was afraid of what he might be thinking. Busybody old man, lives on TV shows, got lucky with a wild guess. Suddenly I thought Steve was going to tell me to forget the whole thing and go home.

Instead he asked me, quite seriously, "Why do you think this subject is dead?"

"Because," I said as carefully as I could, "somebody has tried very hard to hide the fact that Swinney was here. And somebody knows that other people will want to know where Swinney is."

Steve listened, but he shook his head. "You're reaching, Hank."

"Maybe, but I don't think so. Swinney didn't just happen to lose his wallet. Some kid didn't just happen to find it and empty it." I shook my head. "Swinney was important for something he had or something he knew. Remember the key, Steve."

By now we were sitting side by side on the rocks, Steve with his cap pushed back, me rubbing my bald spot where the sun had gotten to it. Steve looked at me thoughtfully.

"Where do you think this alleged body might be found?"

I had given this some thought; I was ready for him. "Remember now, this person, the killer, is careless, an amateur. He's got a body on his hands, or rather, in his car. Maybe he's panicky because he didn't pick a better time and place, or because pretty soon he will be missed from wherever it is he's supposed to be. Maybe he thinks of Lake Champlain. Certainly not far away and certainly deep enough. But this time of year the boat launches are crowded and he's sure to be seen.

"The Civil War iron mines around Palmer Hill are less than an hour from here, but you can't drive right up to the old shafts. You would have to carry or drag the body a long way. That would take time, and there's always the chance of being seen. Then he thinks of the old granite quarry on Route 9 below Ausable Forks. Once you move a couple of sawhorses out of your way, you can drive up pretty close, and one pit is full of water. A few rocks in the pockets and that's the last anyone would ever see of Mr. Thomas Swinney."

Steve tugged on his cap. "We've got no real solid reason to think Swinney was killed around here." I was glad he said "we." "I don't have much to take to the lieutenant or the BCI."

I knew that meant the Bureau of Criminal Investigation. "Look, Steve," I said earnestly, "you've got a known felon, disappeared under suspicious circumstances, probably connected to the narcotics trade."

"What makes you think that?"

"It figures. Boosting cars and running dope go hand in hand. I read the papers."

"It's not very much," Steve said, "but I'll lay it out for the lieutenant." He stood up and started toward his trooper car. "Is there anything else, Hank?"

The sun was hot and I was tired. "Yes, drive me home, will you? It's time for my nap."

The next morning I got an early start. I climbed a fence and went cross-country, carrying an old pair of binoculars. I wanted to check on something at the Page place. In half an hour I was strolling along the highway as usual. I heard a car behind me and hoped it might be Lana Turner. I had missed seeing her yesterday.

It was Steve. He motioned for me to get in the front seat with him. "The Wilmington patrol picked up a body early this morning," he told me.

"Was it Swinney?"

"It was him." Steve tapped the radio. "They just got confirmation on his fingerprints."

I tried hard to appear casual. "So he went for a swim in the quarry."

"Nope," Steve said. "He was high and dry." I twisted around to face him and saw him grinning at me.

"Relax, Hank. You were close enough. A couple of geology students found the body on the road into the quarry late yesterday, and they phoned it in."

Steve told me the students had been prospecting around when they saw a car dump something and drive off. Apparently the driver saw them and got panicky. The students couldn't identify the car or the driver.

"How was Swinney killed?"

"Blow on the head. Something like a jack handle or a poker. Dead about two days, like you figured."

"Anything in his pockets that might indicate what he was doing here?"

Steve shook his head. "A pair of needle-nose pliers and some short pieces of electrical wire. Stuff you might use to hot-wire a car. He must have been good at that."

From the way he was looking at me I realized Steve was holding something back. "Come on, Steve. What else have you got?"

"You remember that safe deposit box key? It was Swinney's, all right, in a Syracuse bank. They got a court order to open it, and guess what they found. Ninety-three thousand dollars in cash."

My mouth dropped open. "Wow! That takes Mr. Swinney out of the bush leagues." I thought about it. "He couldn't make that kind of money stealing cars, could he?" Steve shook his head. "Then there's your narcotics connection, Steve."

"Yep. We thought of that."

We drove along slowly. The sun was already hot, and the top of Whiteface Mountain gleamed in the distance. I was afraid that at any minute the radio would send Steve off on other business, and I had something else to throw at him.

"Steve, you remember you said those New Jersey plates belonged to a blue two-door Dodge Diplomat? Well, I know where that car is. It's in the field behind the Page place."

He frowned at me. "You couldn't possibly know where that individual car is, Hank."

"Hear me out now. This morning I sneaked around there with this pair of glasses. That Dodge is sitting there right now."

Steve shook his head. "They probably built fifty thousand of that model and in that color scheme."

"So what?"

"It would be stupid to keep a hot car right there on the place."

"What better place to keep a stolen car than in a field of other cars? And especially if you plan to use it again."

Steve was deliberately dragging his feet. "You'd have to check the vehicle serial number to know it was the same car."

"Then you'll need a search warrant, won't you?"

He looked at me without speaking and I was afraid I had pushed too hard, but I kept on. This police business was exhilarating; I couldn't stop.

"You're not just looking for a stolen Dodge, Steve. Tell your lieutenant you're looking for a car that's been used to carry cocaine across the border. Maybe bring cash back into the States.

"During Prohibition they used to take the seats out of those big old Packards and Studebakers to bring

down cases of scotch from Canada. Now they're running cocaine up and hiding it in spare tires and seat
cushions and under the hood..."

"I know all that," Steve interrupted.

"That pair of pliers and electrical wire they found
on Swinney. What does that suggest? Maybe he had figured out a new hiding place in a car. Not the radio,
that's too small, but maybe the stereo speakers. Pull
them out, stash the dope in the space, put the covers
back on..."

Steve looked at me appraisingly. "You're guessing
again, Hank. I admit you've been guessing pretty good,
but you're guessing."

I was feeling so good I was absolutely reckless. "It's
called deduction, Officer Marion. Basic deduction."

"Speculation," he said. "Pure and simple speculation." He put his hands on the wheel. "I've got to go.
Drive you home?"

"No, thanks. I need the exercise. Tell me, Steve, are
you going to try for a warrant?"

"I'll see what the drug enforcement boys say.
Chance are they'll go for it. And to tell you the truth,
Hank, that Page outfit has been known to dabble in
stolen cars. They chop them up for parts." He reached
for the ignition key. "I'll be in touch."

"Hang on a minute." There was something on my
mind, and I had to speak up now.

"Steve, there's a young lady who lives on the Page
place. Some kind of distant cousin, I think. She seems
like a nice girl, and I don't think she could possibly have
anything to do with whatever might be going on over
there." I paused and glanced at Steve. He sat quietly,
waiting for me to finish. "Anyway, I feel sorry for her.
Old Mrs. Page can't be much company for her, and

there she is, a single, attractive young girl there with a hardshell uncle and that young stud Walt Junior..."

Steve held up his hand to stop me. "Who are you, Tennessee Williams? I get the picture." He grinned but it was an understanding grin. "All right, if we go in for a look around, I'll keep her out of it."

"Thanks, Steve."

I got out and he drove away. Now I felt better. I couldn't protect Lana Turner myself, but Steve had said he would look out for her. This detective work might be fun, but I wouldn't want to create any problems for the pretty young woman with a kind smile for an old man. I felt so good I walked an extra mile on the way home.

Things moved fast after that. The next morning Steve said, "We got the warrant to search the Page place. The lieutenant says he'll have my hide if we come up empty."

"Don't worry. Tell him I'll help write up your commendation."

"Some drug enforcement boys will be here at noon. We'll go in then." Steve was perfectly relaxed; I hadn't been so excited in years. A real police raid, just like in the movies.

"About the raid, Steve," I said, trying to sound as calm as he did, "will I be issued a sidearm, or am I going in strictly as an observer? Could I bring a camera along?"

Steve just stared straight ahead through the windshield. I wondered why he didn't answer my question, and I was about to repeat it.

"You've been a big help on this thing, Hank," he said finally. I noticed his face was getting red. "But you can't go with us."

I couldn't go? I was stunned. It was like a kick in the stomach. Of course they didn't want an old man along. Get out of the way, let the professionals take over. This is the real world; who needs a has-been schoolteacher. My own face got red. I opened the door and stepped out.

"Wait a minute, Hank."

"Save it, Steve," I snapped. I was furious but I was more hurt than mad. I had trouble breathing. I started down the side of the road and Steve followed me.

"Hold it, Hank. Please." I stopped and turned around. There was a strained look on Steve's young face. "Hank, take away thirty years and you'd be a great partner."

All right, it wasn't his fault. This was police work, and I was a civilian. "Thanks, Steve." I started down the road. "See you around, son."

Then a giant belt cinched itself around my chest and choked the breath out of me and a thousand needles stabbed into my left arm. The sky tilted violently and I blacked out. I think Steve caught me before I hit the pavement.

I didn't know anything else for three days. Steve got me to a hospital in time, and the repair work on my heart was successful. I won't be walking so much any more, but Steve and I are planning to do some fishing real soon. He told me the details of what I missed.

The troopers and the federal agents had their raid on the Page property and found things pretty much as Steve and I predicted. The DEA knew the crime families were delivering cocaine into Canada by concealing it in automobiles. They brought the cash payments down the same way. The families didn't trust each other completely, so they switched cars and cargoes frequently on the run from Florida to Canada and back again.

The Page place was just one of many transfer spots. Drivers were changed frequently, too, and that's where Thomas Swinney came on board. He made a number of trips between the Page place and other points in New Jersey and Pennsylvania. The spare license plates were just tools of the trade. Swinney had made a lot of money and bragged about it, and that got him killed. By Walt Junior, who was jealous of Swinney's attentions to Lana Turner.

I guess I was wrong about her. Her real name was Judy something. She had a husband doing eight to twelve years in Dannemora. She was the real boss of the Page operation; the mob had planted her there to protect its interests, and she made a lot of the runs into Canada.

It seems she hated the mountains and she elected Thomas Swinney and his bankroll to be her ticket out of the boondocks. But one night up at the turnout, Walt Junior dissolved the partnership with a piece of angle iron. He searched for a clue to Swinney's money, but he was careless and didn't find the key. He and his father and an uncle are out on bail, awaiting trial.

So is the pretty young woman who reminded me so much of my college dream girl, Lana Turner. I can still see that bright blonde hair and that warm open smile. I can't believe I was entirely wrong about her. Anyone that pretty can't be all bad.

So long, Lana Turner. It was nice knowing you.

Four
Hundred
Pieces of
Cheese

Trooper Kim Newcomb looked around, frowning. She was surrounded by hundreds of slot machines. They were stacked three high in dozens of neat precise rows. They took up almost half the floor space in the police impound warehouse.

Kim and her boss, Station Sergeant Fuller, stood in a narrow center aisle. "Let me get this straight," Kim said. "I'm supposed to load up all four hundred of these things and haul them sixty miles just to have them destroyed? This is a joke, right?"

Fuller shook his head, the overhead light gleaming on his bald spot. "No joke. That's the assignment."

Kim was still skeptical. As the only female officer in the State Police station in Malone she had been the

After The Summer People Leave

target of much unfunny male humor. She had learned to watch her step, in and out of the patrol room.

"So why not destroy them right here?" she asked. "Run them over with a bulldozer or something?"

Fuller shook his head. "Not good enough."

"Dig a hole and bury them?"

"No good. The D.A. wants these slots run through a car crusher in Plattsburgh."

"Then why not have a moving company pick them up and deliver them?"

Fuller was impatient. The morning shift change was over and the station was quiet but a lot of work waited for him on his desk.

"Because, Newcomb," he said evenly, "these damn things are worth a lot of money and some bad men with guns might just try to steal them. Get the picture now?"

Kim's face reddened. "Oh. Oh, I see." A strand of blonde hair escaped from the tight bun at the base of her neck; quickly she tucked it back into place. Kim wore very little make-up, aware that Captain Banks had said she was almost too pretty to be a trooper, that people wouldn't take her seriously.

"Look, Newcomb," Fuller said, "I know you just got assigned here from the Academy in Albany and maybe you don't know the background here.

"We confiscated these slots from the casinos on the Akwesasne reservation at St. Regis about three years ago. The Mohawks were having something of a civil war over the issue of gambling. Slot machines are illegal in New York, you know."

Fuller turned and led the way to the door at the end of the warehouse. "We've had to hold the machines here as evidence, but now the D.A. has closed the case and the slots have to be destroyed."

Kim nodded. He was right, of course. Cocaine, marijuana, slots, whatever, if it was illegal it had to be destroyed. Not buried or hidden but burned or smashed out of existence. But does Fuller really think that some criminals might try to take these things off our hands?

The door opened and an older man in civilian clothes stood there, smiling. From the way he shook hands with Fuller, Kim knew they were old friends.

Fuller introduced her. "Kim Newcomb, this is Captain Mark Benjamin. He's BCI."

Automatically Kim snapped to attention with a hand salute. The agent returned it. "Trooper Newcomb," he said, "a pleasure."

Mark Benjamin had a disarming smile and a gentle voice. He looked like a successful broker or realtor. He was dressed in a dapper three-piece suit, with a silk square in the pocket. Kim had to remind herself that he was a lawman.

"Glad to know you, Captain Benjamin," she said.

Fuller turned back to her. "All right, Kim," he said, "here's the plan as approved by the D.A. and Captain Banks. You take these slots to the Champlain Salvage Company in West Plattsburgh. They've got a big car crusher, the only one in the north country.

"You witness the slots being destroyed and certify that to the D.A. The county sells what's left for scrap and that's the end of it. And good riddance.

"Clear your plans with Captain Benjamin here. He can give you a hand with transport or whatever." Fuller turned to go. "Another thing, Newcomb. I've detailed Dean Edmond to work with you."

Dean Edmond! Kim opened her mouth but Fuller was gone. Of all the other troopers in the station Edmond would have been her last choice. A young, self-impressed macho-male type. She would give odds that it was Edmond who put the dead mouse in her locker or tied about a hundred knots in her shoelaces.

She gritted her teeth. Go along to get along, she told herself. Mark Benjamin was watching her, an amused expression on his face. Kim turned away and stepped over to the nearest stack of slot machines.

On impulse she dropped a quarter in the slot and tugged the handle. Immediately she heard the characteristic whir and clack of the three wheels as they spun behind the glass window.

She looked up in surprise. "These things still work!"

"Evidence," said Mark. "They had to be kept intact just the way they were brought in." He ran his fingers over the front of the machine; it was heavily embossed with an intricate design of eagles and flags. "The original one-armed bandit," he said. "These things are the backbone of a casino operation."

Kim nodded in agreement. She knew that most people have never actually seen a roulette wheel or know all the rules of poker or blackjack. But everybody knows how to feed coins into a slot machine.

"Aren't there newer models out now?" she asked.

"Yes, indeed," answered Mark. "There are new electronic games but these standard manual types are still worth a few hundred dollars a copy."

"You think the Mohawks might try to get them back?"

He shook his head. "The tribe is close to an agreement with the Gaming Commission down in Albany. It wouldn't do to rock the boat. But there are ready markets for these things. The gaming states like New Jersey. Over a hundred Indian casinos around the country. Country clubs and Legion halls everywhere."

Kim needed time to think. She turned to the door. "How about a cup of coffee, Captain?"

"Sold."

Outside the warehouse Kim stopped and held up her hand. There was the faint but unmistakable sound of geese flying overhead. She searched the sky and spotted them, a long wavering vee formation. Autumn was almost over in upstate New York; thousands of geese had already flown south to escape the snows soon to come. This would be Kim's first winter here; she took the assignment to be near her grandmother, who was ill.

The impound warehouse was a large steel structure at the rear of the station, an attractive red brick building on the east side of Malone. A driveway ran from the street back to the warehouse and an adjoining service garage.

"You folks need some help here?" It was Trooper Edmond. He was tall and lean, and quite handsome in his uniform.

"Hi, Newcomb," he said to Kim with a grin. Around the station he called her "junior" and treated her as if she were still in pigtails. Kim introduced him to Mark Benjamin politely. "Come and join us for coffee," she said.

They found seats at a small table in the patrol room. Mark sat across from Kim, completely at ease. Kim stared at her cup, thinking. What was a captain in the Bureau of Criminal Investigation doing here? He didn't just drop by to say hello. That office handled only major crimes.

"So, Captain Benjamin," she said, leaning toward him, "do you think someone is going to make a try for these slots? Is that why you're here?"

He grinned at her. "You guessed it, Trooper."

He glanced around casually. "You both know there's been some big-time highway heists up here lately, trailers loaded with liquor, electronic gear, big-ticket stuff. It's a gang of highway pirates with a first-class distribution setup behind them."

"And you want to use the slots as bait?"

Mark smiled gently. "Right again, Kim. Bait to catch some troublesome rats."

Dean had been listening open-mouthed. He turned to Kim. "Hold on here. Our job is to get the damn things to the salvage company, not to play games with them."

He looked from Kim to Mark. "Look, we simply set up a convoy. Load the slots into trucks, put two troop cars in front and two in back. Nobody in his right mind would tackle a setup like that."

Mark looked at Kim. "Any other ideas?" he asked quietly.

She stood up and walked to the window. Across the paved area in the rear was the service garage. To the left and surrounded by a high fence was the vehicle impound area. As usual several vehicles were inside, seized for various offenses.

Fuller did me a favor by giving me this job, she thought. I've got to show some initiative. Dean's plan is simple and foolproof all right but Captain Benjamin wants to get criminals off the street, and that's the game we're paid to play. She turned back to the table.

"It's common knowledge that we're holding the machines here, right?"

"Right."

"And it's known they're not needed now for evidence?"

"Right. It was in the paper."

Kim frowned. "So somebody could be over there across the street watching the warehouse right now, waiting for us to make a move."

Mark nodded. "I'd bet the farm on it."

Kim looked out the window again, at the vehicles beyond the impound fence. There was a laundry van that said MOTHER'S HELPER on the side. Kim knew it had been confiscated because it had been transporting marijuana instead of diapers.

"All right," she said suddenly, "if someone is waiting to see us load up these slots we won't disappoint him."

She turned to Mark. "Can you get us a big moving van, like Allied and Mayflower use?"

"Sure. Say when."

"And some muscle for loading?"

"Any time."

Kim took a deep breath. "All right. We'll set out the bait. Today is Thursday. We'll need tomorrow to get ready. We could go on Saturday." She looked at Mark. "How does this sound, Captain?"

Immediately Dean shook his head and said, "Suppose it doesn't work?"

Kim whirled to face him. "Then it's my badge and my butt, all right?" She turned to Mark Benjamin. "Sorry, sir. Any comments?"

Mark was grinning at her. "Good plan. Let's do it."

For the first time that day Kim smiled. "Thank you, sir," she said. "After all, four hundred pieces of cheese ought to catch some good-sized rats, am I right?"

"Right," said Mark.

"I guess so," said Dean.

On Friday morning a Bronco towing a large horse trailer was driven down the driveway and into the vehicle impound area. Any interested observer would assume that the vehicles were guilty of some violation. Meanwhile they sat alongside the laundry van.

In the afternoon a Franklin County sand truck limped down the driveway and stopped in front of the service garage. The driver busied himself under the hood for a few minutes, then abandoned the big truck and departed on foot.

But on Saturday morning an observer would have been amused by the sight of a large moving van inching its way in reverse down the driveway. Following a trooper's hand signals it backed toward the warehouse. It eased into position parallel to the building with its rear doors as close as possible to the warehouse door. A ramp was erected between the two doors.

Mark Benjamin had arranged for a work crew from the Bare Hill Correctional Facility outside Malone; ten men dressed in drab prison garb were present. Hand trucks appeared and the men began the task of moving the slot machines from the warehouse into the van. A trooper with a clipboard tallied the machines as they passed along the ramp.

The men maintained a steady pace. In less than two hours the last of the machines went aboard and the doors were closed and locked. A uniformed trooper took his place behind the wheel, another beside him.

Slowly the van went up the driveway and turned into the street. It headed west on Route 11. An observer would have been quite interested to note that the van traveled alone, with no trooper escort.

Kim and Mark Benjamin stepped out of the center door of the warehouse. They were joined by Dean Edmond and three off-duty officers. They were all in casual clothes as part of Kim's plan. She wore jeans and a leather jacket, her blonde hair concealed under a baseball cap. As usual Mark was dressed almost formally in civilian clothes.

"You think someone out there will take the bait?" asked Dean.

"Don't worry, my boy," said Mark, "the old hat trick never fails."

"Let's saddle up," Kim said. "There's no time to waste." She was praying her plan would work. If it did she would be a member of the club, not just the new transfer from downstate. No more being the first name called for funeral escort details or domestic dispute calls at two o'clock in the morning.

One of the officers walked over and unlocked the gate of the impound area. Inside, three large vehicles were parked facing the driveway; the horse trailer, the laundry van and the sand truck. All three sagged under the combined weight of four hundred slot machines.

The moving van was a decoy. A watcher would have seen the prisoners loading slot machines into the rear of the van. He would not have known that Mark Benjamin had procured a van with a side door, a door on its right side. The slots had been wheeled out of this door and back into the warehouse. Inside again they were taken through the building, behind the service garage, and loaded into the three waiting vehicles.

The van had been sent on its way empty of cargo. Aboard were members of a Mobile Response Team, armed and ready for any interference by the highway pirates that Captain Benjamin hoped to capture.

"Dean and I will lead off with the Bronco," Kim said. Dean had been critical about her plan, but he had cooperated. He had even borrowed the horse trailer from an uncle's horse farm. Kim promised herself that when this was over she would keep her distance from him.

She turned to Mark. "You still want to go, sir?" He was near retirement age; there was no need for him to make this trip.

"Try and stop me," Mark answered.

"All right, you go with Harry in the laundry truck. You other guys drive the county truck. Give us a ten-minute head start."

She glanced at Dean. "Hop in. I'll drive."

Route 374 was the most direct route to Morrison-ville and West Plattsburgh. It wound through the steep grades and desolate country around Lyon Mountain. The barren trees and lifeless fields were depressing to Kim; so different from the urban areas she was used to.

Cheer up, kid, Kim said to herself. You had a good idea. Benjamin thought so and Fuller went along. So what if you are the new kid on the block?

Now she had left the village of Dannemora far behind and the salvage yard was just two miles ahead. Dean was dozing in his seat, snoring gently. Kim began to frown; something else was nagging at her.

Fuller was right; these slots were a pain in the rear. They couldn't be buried or dumped in the river; they had to be physically destroyed. They had to be brought here and fed to a car crusher. This one. The only car crusher in the north country.

So anybody who knew the law and who had any acquisitive interest in the machines could figure out this is where the machines would wind up, courtesy of the state police!

"Damn!" She slammed her fist against the steering wheel. Here she was, sitting on the cheese, but was she taking it into a trap? A trap just waiting for her to show up?

Ahead she saw a sign that read "Champlain Salvage Company" hanging over big double gates of the entrance. She punched Dean hard on the shoulder. "Wake up!"

He stirred and opened his eyes.

"Listen up, Dean," Kim said rapidly. "This morning we pretended to send out some bait and hoped the rats would follow it, right? But how many rats are there that want this cheese? Maybe right now we're bringing it to some rats we don't know about! You follow me?"

She was at the gate of the salvage yard. On either side of the driveway were ugly hills of junked cars and bales of rusty scrap metal. As she wheeled the Bronco inside a man came out of the watchman's shack by the side of the gate and hurried toward them.

"Get down!" Kim hit Dean on the shoulder and pushed him roughly to the floor.

"What are you going to do?"

"Stay down! This may be a reception committee. Don't let him see you!"

She pulled the Bronco forward so the horse trailer cleared the gate and braked to a stop. Behind her the man was shouting. Kim stepped out and slammed the door and walked forward to meet him. On impulse she took off her baseball cap and shook her hair loose; she hoped it would give her a disarming appearance.

"You can't bring that rig in here!" the man said angrily. He was in his forties, with a white, beefy face and a middle that had handled too much beer. "Turn around and get those horses out of here!"

Defiantly Kim put her hands on her hips. "This is the Champlain Salvage Company, isn't it?"

"Yeah. Who wants to know?" The man looked at her suspiciously, one hand moving toward a bulge under his windbreaker.

"Where's the boss?" Kim demanded in a haughty tone. "I've got a load of slot machines here, buster."

The man glared from her to the horse trailer. "In that?" Kim ignored his scowl and gave him a big smile.

Go for it, girl, she told herself, keep him off balance. She reached out and patted the side of the trailer.

"You were expecting maybe a moving van with maybe a couple of cops, right?" She put her hand on the latch of the trailer door. "We switched to keep the shipment a secret. Cute, ain't it?"

She lifted the top half of the door. The man stepped closer and stared at the slot machines jumbled inside. Kim almost laughed at the expression on his face.

"Slots, by God!" He backed away and looked toward the yard office. "All right, sister. Drive down there." He pointed to the rear of the yard.

"Not so fast, buster," Kim said. She closed the door and took a step toward the man. "Let's get one thing straight." She took another step and peered up into his face.

"I'll tell you like I told that sergeant back in Malone. I don't load and I don't unload. All I do is drive." She took another step closer. "I just drive. You see what I'm saying, mister?"

He's on the defensive now, Kim thought. Talk his ears off and he won't be able to think.

"All right, sister, don't push. Just drive down there."

Kim shook her head. "Not so fast." She waved the ignition key in his face. "Not until I get my money. I'm not moving this trailer another foot until I get paid. One hundred and twenty dollars. Now you tell the boss to come up with my money."

She moved closer and the man retreated, clearly exasperated. He looked up again at the old trailer that must have been the yard office. Kim continued her refrain.

"If I was you, mister," she said, "I'd make some room in the driveway. My cousin is right behind me with another load, and she'll want her money, too."

"Another load?"

Kim nodded, her blonde hair flying. "And you can tell the boss she doesn't load and unload. We just drive. You see what I'm saying?"

"All right, already! Over here!" The man led the way to the old trailer. Still talking, Kim followed him.

The man opened the door and waved her inside. Two men were seated at a large desk playing gin rummy. There were a shotgun and a pistol on the desk. The men looked up as they entered.

"Hey, Mike," said the man, "this dame just pulled in with a load of those slots and she says there's another load..."

The older of the two men threw down his cards. "You dummy! How do you know she ain't a cop?"

"She is a cop," said Dean. He stood in the doorway with his gun leveled at the two men. "Now everybody stand real still."

"Real still," echoed Kim, her gun out from under her jacket and covering the phony watchman. "Real still."

An hour later the salvage yard was bustling with activity. The real watchman had been found bound and gagged in a tool shed. Now he was being interviewed by a Channel Five news team. The three men had been turned over to troopers from the Plattsburgh station.

The yard foreman had been called and in turn had summoned a crew to operate the big crusher, the overtime to be billed to Franklin County. Conveyors had been set up to move the slots from the vehicles to the bed of the machine. En route they passed over a scale; the final weight of the compressed scrap would match this total.

In an ear-splitting crunch the crusher devoured ten slot machines at a time, ending forever the temptations of easy money and high profits.

"You should have been here, Captain," Dean said to Mark Benjamin. "You should have seen Kim fake that guy out. She was great!"

"I'm sorry I missed it."

"Those guys could have had us flat-footed but at the last minute Kim thought something was wrong. It was her show all the way."

They joined Kim where she was monitoring the crusher at work. "I just talked to Fuller," Mark told her. "The decoy paid off. Two guys tried to take down the van just outside Brushton. They tried a fake accident as a roadblock but it didn't work. They're in custody."

"Good," Kim said. "Were they the pirates you were hoping to catch?"

Mark shook his head. "No. These were just amateurs who have been robbing convenience stores around Essex County. They thought boosting the slot machines would be a career move."

"Oh, I see." She tried to sound casual but there was disappointment in her voice. So her plan hadn't worked.

Then she saw Mark smiling at her and glimpsed Dean turning away to hide a grin.

"But you did hit the jackpot, Kim," Mark said. "Right here. Those bozos you and Dean collared are the real bad boys. They were pretty smart to dope out the connection between the slot machines and the car crusher here. All they had to do was stake out this place."

"But they weren't smart enough," Dean cut in, grinning. "Somebody phoned them; they were expecting the van."

"Right," Kim said, frowning again. "We should have figured it. If there was one person watching the warehouse, why not two? We weren't very bright."

Mark laughed. "Bright enough, young lady." He held out his hand. "Next time you have a few hundred pieces of cheese, call me. We'll catch some more rats."

Mark gave her a friendly pat on the shoulder, then he waved to both of them, and was gone.

Dean moved closer to her. Instinctively Kim stepped back. "Don't get any ideas," she said warningly.

He shook his head. "Listen, Kim," he said. "I'm sorry about all the dumb stuff the guys did to you. I'll make sure there won't be any more." He looked at her beseechingly. "All right?"

"Sure," said Kim. "And drop the big brother act."

"You got it." Dean held up his right hand, palm out. "How about if I call you partner?"

Kim smiled and raised her right hand and slapped it into his.

"Why not," she said, "partner."

The Trouble on Brown Island

The water was icy. Dale Whitetree shivered as he clung to one of the floating blue drums at the side of the trout pen. And he was painfully out of condition for swimming underwater. But if he was going to find the guns he would have to search the bottom and the water here was ten feet deep.

"You really think they threw those machine guns in here?" he had asked Barney Watt, the ATF agent.

The older man nodded. "Be a great place to hide something," he said, "under ten thousand fish."

A steady breeze ruffled the water; they couldn't see the bottom from where they stood on the catwalk. And time was short; if the guns were here the smugglers could be on their way across the St. Lawrence and back to the island at this very minute. And Brown Island belonged to the Akwesasne Mohawks, it had to be protected.

"I'll take a look," Dale said. He stripped to his shorts and dived in.

He filled his lungs and swam down. The water stung his eyes; he wished there had been time to at least get a face mask. Dimly he could make out clumps of weeds and large stones. His foot struck the bottom and sent up a cloud of sediment, blinding him. He stroked up to the surface, panting.

He moved a few feet farther along the row of drums and tried again. This time he used the wire netting on the side of the pen to pull himself down. A small trout looked at him curiously, then flicked its tail and darted away. Dale had seen perhaps a hundred trout hovering in the shadow of the catwalk, a tiny fraction of what had been here yesterday.

Was it vandals who had cut the netting and allowed the fish to escape, or smugglers trying to recover the contraband intended for Canada? He had to find out.

Dale shot to the surface and shook his head at Barney and the other men watching from the dock. "Nothing yet."

Barney had told him the guns were probably packed two in a bundle. "They'll be wrapped in plastic, a little water wouldn't hurt." And by now the current of the river would have covered the bundles with a fine silt.

Dale took a deep breath and pulled himself down again. This time he saw something, an irregular shape outlined against the bottom. He propelled himself toward it and touched it with his foot. It felt slippery and heavy. His lungs about to burst, he prodded the object with his hand and it moved.

He surfaced, gasping. "Something down there. I need a rope." Ross threw him a coil of light line, a slip knot in one end to form a noose.

On his fourth try Dale managed to get the rope around what might be a bundle of the machine guns. His lungs rebelled before he reached the surface and he swallowed a huge quantity of water. Ross helped him out on the catwalk and he lay there, retching and panting, as Barney and Lee carefully pulled up the object he had found on the bottom.

Less than two hours ago Dale had been sitting peacefully in his office in the tribe's new Community Building. The sign on his desk read "Assistant Director." The sign was new; Dale had graduated from the state university in Potsdam, New York, in May.

Patsy, the Division secretary, came in the door, a serious expression on her face. "Just got a message from Ross," she told him. "'Tell Rory Horn there's trouble on Brown Island.'"

Horn was Dale's boss and Director of the Mohawks' Environment Division. But Horn was out of town, in Washington for an EPA symposium; therefore any problem was Dale's problem, especially if it was on Brown Island.

Dale jumped to his feet. "I'll go see what's going on," he said. "Hold the fort, will you?"

"Right," Patsy said. "Lee Bassett will meet you at the dock in St. Regis."

"Corporal Lee Bassett? Are the police in on this?"

"Yes," Patsy answered, "they got the same message."

Dale left his office running.

Lee Bassett was several years older than Dale but they both had the classic Mohawk profile with the strong nose and heavy chin and thick black hair. Lee wore the midnight blue uniform of the St. Regis Mohawk Police.

"Too bad your boss is out of town," Lee said. "Brown Island is his baby, isn't it?"

"Right," Dale answered. But it's my baby today, he thought. "Let's take our boat," he said. "It's faster."

Ten minutes later they were running past the eastern end of Cornwall island, the August sun burning away the morning mists. Ahead were the small channel islands scattered in the mighty St. Lawrence. One of these was Brown Island, the site of the Mohawks' fish farm, a project of the tribe's Environment Division.

The fish farm was an answer to the plague of pollution on the reservation. For generations the Mohawks had existed by hunting and fishing and farming. Then came giant manufacturing plants on the west side of the reservation, dumping PCBs into the waterways, spewing contaminants into the air.

Within a few years the Raquette and St. Regis Rivers on the reservation became dangerously polluted; fishing had to be banned. Under the supervision of the Environment Division the tribe began raising rainbow trout. Rory Horn had secured a grant to finance the project; the work had been done by volunteers. This fall fresh, clean fish would again be a part of the Mohawks' diet.

Now Dale could see Brown Island ahead. It was small, uninhabited, covered with pine and birch and a peculiar dusty fern that gave the island its name.

Here in a narrow inlet the fish farm had been constructed. Wire netting was suspended in the water from rows of watertight plastic drums. The enclosure was some thirty feet square, held in place by cables from trees on shore. The pond had been stocked with fingerling trout purchased from hatcheries in upstate New York. There were close to ten thousand fish; with daily feeding they would soon be large enough to harvest.

Inside the bay a dock and storage shed had been built along the shoreline. Dale brought his boat alongside another boat tied up at the dock.

A tall Indian was waiting for them. Ross Talkstone was an elder of the tribe; he was as lean as a pine, with long grey hair held in place by a headband. Silently he pointed at the fish pen.

Dale gasped, not believing his eyes. Where there should have been a shimmering mass of silver fish the water was empty. The thousands of little trout were gone; only the rows of floating drums remained.

"What happened?" Dale asked.

"Come, I'll show you."

A floating catwalk reached from the dock to the holding pen. Other narrow catwalks extended across the pen for use in feeding the small fish.

Ross stepped out on a row of the drums. They bobbed and danced under his weight but he kept his balance effortlessly. On the side of the square facing the river he stopped and pointed at a section of netting beneath him.

The wire had been cut from the surface almost to the bottom, allowing the fish to escape into the river. Ross had pulled the opening together again, lacing the edges with twine.

Ross led the way back to the dock. "I came to feed the fish as usual," he said. "Whoever did this must have heard my boat or seen me coming. He took off in his own boat. A white man, a small open boat.

"I saw fish streaming out of the cut he had made. I tied the netting together as best I could and sent my grandson in with the message." He paused and Dale saw the look of anger on the older man's face. "I wish I could have caught that man."

"No idea of who he was?" Lee asked quietly.

Ross shook his head. "Too far away."

"He left in a hurry all right," Lee said. "Forgot his hat." He pointed at a cheap cloth hat stuck on one of the pilings that supported the dock.

Dale barely heard him. He was thinking of the loss to the tribe the damage had caused. The days of planning, the weeks of effort, now wasted. And it would be up to him to tell Rory the bad news.

"This is the worst case of vandalism I've ever heard of!" he burst out angrily.

Lee was looking out at the river. "Maybe it isn't vandalism," he said slowly.

Dale and Ross stared at him. "What do you mean?"

Lee propped a foot on a bench by the shed. "You guys got any idea of how much smuggling takes place on this part of the St. Lawrence? You know it's the boundary between New York and Canada."

"We know that, Lee," Dale answered. The river actually divided the Mohawk reservation; Hogansburg in New York and Cornwall in Canada. "What are you getting at?"

"The river is mighty big and it's damn hard to patrol. Liquor and tobacco are the big ticket items going up into Canada; illegal aliens and counterfeit currency come south. Take my word for it, the contraband runs into millions. But the thing is, some of the parties in the smuggling business use little islands like this one as meeting places, or places to hide."

"I hear gunfire at night," Ross said quietly, "and I know it isn't duck hunters."

"You got that right," Lee said. "Some of these guys get greedy and hijack each others' cargoes. Or they try to outrun a Customs patrol, which usually is a big mistake."

"So what?" Dale pointed at the netting. "Ruining our holding pen is still vandalism, no matter who did it. Look, I've got to get back to town. I've got to call Rory, and I ought to call Chief Solomon, and..."

Lee had turned away and was staring out at the river again. Dale realized he had been hearing the sound of a motor; he turned and saw a small boat rounding the point, heading for the dock.

"I know this fellow," Lee told them. "I called him on the radio when we got here. He can tell you better than I can what's going on."

The man who joined them on the dock was white, clean-shaven, dressed casually. He was in his late fifties and moved stiffly as he climbed out of his boat. Dale notice he wore a belt radio similar to Lee's.

Lee made the introductions. "Dale Whitetree, Ross Talkstone, this is Barney Watt."

The man held out his hand, first to Ross, then to Dale. "Sekon skenenko wa," he said.

In answer Ross made a traditional Mohawk sign of greeting. The white man had addressed them in the Mohawk language. Dale was impressed; it was an uncommon gesture of respect.

Barney Watt surveyed the damaged netting. "I'm sorry about the loss of your stock," he said politely. To Lee he said, "It's a good thing you called me. We better talk."

They sat on benches by the shed. "Barney here is an agent with the ATF," Lee said. "He works with Canadian Customs."

"ATF," Ross said. "Alcohol, Tobacco and Firearms. What's that got to do with our fish?"

Barney leaned forward. "Most of the big-time smuggling on the river is east of here, up toward Summertown, where they run big boats with big cargos. But a certain group is using this part of the river to run fire-arms into Canada. You're out of the main traffic here, and this armament is small, easy to handle in small boats."

Dale shook his head. An ATF agent interested in what happened on Brown Island was more bad news for Rory. He looked out at the small bay, sparkling in the sunlight, at the rows of blue drums bobbing gently in the water. The fish farm project is ruined, he thought, and smuggling hasn't got anything to do with our work in the Division. But he was intrigued by the agent's story.

"What kind of firearms are they?" Dale asked.

Barney had a small case beside his feet. He opened it and took out a strange-looking gun. It was shaped like a letter T with the handle protruding from the center of a barrel fashioned from square black tubing. "You know what this is?" he asked.

"A pretty big pistol," Dale answered.

"It's more than a pistol," Barney said. "It's a machine gun. This is a SWD M-Eleven, nine millimeter. We see a lot of these in our business.

"You can buy this legally for four or five hundred dollars. It comes semi-automatic, but it can easily be converted to full automatic. That makes it a machine gun, and it's totally illegal. Now you sell the weapon for fifteen hundred, or more. A pretty good profit, and there's a steady demand."

"And they sell them right here on the river?"

"We've got an informant on the other side," Barney said. "We know one night a week two men, we think they're from the Fort Covington area, bring a few of these guns out to an island in the river.

"The rendezvous point is set up in advance. They don't want to meet in the open water; they might attract attention from a patrol or from other operators. At the island they meet the boat with the money and make the exchange. That's the way it works, up until two nights ago."

"Let me guess," said Lee, "something went wrong."

"Yep. A sting had been set up. An undercover agent in Canada put in a big order, for thirty guns, and the plan was to make the arrest after the delivery. But something happened.

"Our man says the Canadian boat with the money was late and the delivery boys got spooked, maybe by a patrol. They decided to hide the guns so if they got picked up they're clean. They stashed the guns on an island, figuring to come back for them a day or so later."

"Lots of islands," Ross said. "Your man say which one?"

Barney looked out at the holding pen in the cove, now empty of fish. "No, but your island sure seems to have somebody's attention."

Dale nodded in agreement. He stepped out on the catwalk and looked down at the water. He could visualize what might have happened that night: two men in a heavily loaded boat, clinging to these pilings, hearing other boats on the river, growing more and more apprehensive. They could be cornered in this cove, arrested or shot, their cargo seized, fifty thousand dollars worth of weapons gone. Finally the men pull their boat along the side of the pen, throw their packages across the netting into the water, and race to safety.

"And when they come back they realize they have to cut the netting to get at the guns," Dale said.

"That's the way I read it," Barney answered. He looked at his watch. "I'm running out of time. I've got to set up some security in case the man that Ross saw comes back, and I've got to locate a diver and some gear."

"We still don't know for sure if the guns are down there," Dale said slowly.

"You're right, young fellow," said Ross. "So far we're just guessing."

"I used to swim a bit," said Dale, "maybe I could take a look."

A big grin creased Barney's face. "I was hoping you'd say that."

"Bingo," said Lee Bassett.

The bundle contained two of the M-Eleven machine guns and half a dozen empty magazines, wrapped all together in brown plastic.

"Nice going, young fellow," said Ross. "You see any more of these packages down there?"

Dale was using his shirt as a towel. "I'm pretty sure I did."

"They're there," Barney said. "Count on it." He looked at his watch again. "Dale, can you stay here and catch your breath until I get back? I've got to get on to the Joint Customs Group in Rouses Point and the Quebec Provincial Police. I'll take the guns in with me as evidence.

"Lee, you run in and contact the state police and the BCI, bring them up to speed. And get back here with some help if you can."

"You got it," said Lee.

Ross untied his boat. "I've got to get some heavy wire to fix that netting."

Five minutes later Dale sat on the dock alone. The sound of the departing boats had faded and the cove was quiet except for the water lapping against the pilings. He watched a pair of belted kingfishers fly low over the water. No more free lunch for you guys, he thought.

Maybe we did lose a lot of fish to the birds, he mused. Maybe we should have put some lightweight netting overhead. And maybe had a guard at night. Too late now; the fish farm is history.

At least some of the other projects for the good of the tribe are working out. The new school building. The Head Start program. The library with books in the Mohawk language. New casinos would bring in revenue for the tribe. And he and Rory and the staff could still work to heal the environment.

The warm sunshine and the exercise were having an effect; Dale's eyes began to close. He glimpsed the shadow of a man standing behind him, an arm raised, swinging down. A burst of pain bloomed in his head and the world was dark. He crumpled to the dock and lay there.

The man behind him put away his gun and began to tie Dale's hands.

"Dale." A quiet voice was repeating his name. It was annoying him. He shook his head but the voice was persistent. "Dale." He opened his eyes but the bright light triggered a stab of pain in his head. He closed his eyes again.

"Dale. Wake up, Dale." This time his eyes stayed open. He saw the edge of a wall of boards and a slice of sky. He turned his head slightly and saw a line of blue drums floating in the water. "Dale." It was Ross, whispering his name.

He realized he was lying on the dock at the corner of the shed, his hands tied behind him. "Don't move, young fellow. Keep your eyes on that clay-head out there."

Dale twisted his head and saw a man on the center catwalk, a beefy, middle-aged white man with a black mustache. Despite the summer heat he wore a long-sleeved wool shirt and was sweating profusely. He was facing away from the dock, drawing a line up out of the water.

Two of them, Dale thought, there were two of them! One man took off; the other hid out somewhere.

"Ross?" he said weakly, his throat dry and tight. "Ross, is that you? I thought you went back to town."

The old Indian reached around the corner of the shed and poured water from a tin cup over Dale's head. It eased the pulsating pain.

"I just went around to the other side of the island," Ross said in a low voice. "Left my boat and came back through the trees to look for the other man. I was up there on the ridge when he sneaked up on you and clubbed you on the head."

Ross tilted another cup of water over Dale's head; the pain was receding.

"What made you think there were two men here this morning?" Dale asked.

"Remember that hat Lee found? The man I saw leaving was wearing a hat. The second hat could have belonged to another man."

"Why didn't you say something?"

"I could have been wrong. Now lie still."

Dale watched the man on the catwalk. There was a grappling hook on the end of his line. He swung it a few times and dropped it in the water. Dale glimpsed a handgun stuck in his belt.

"Untie me, Ross," Dale whispered, "before that guy's partner comes back."

"Just sit tight, young fellow, I'll take care of him."

"But he's got a gun."

"I know. Give me a minute and then call him over here."

The man on the catwalk was tugging on his line; it was snagged on the bottom. Dale could hear him cursing.

Dale tried his voice. "Hey, you! You out there!"

The man heard him and turned around. He could see Dale was still helplessly tied. He yanked on his line again and then dropped it in disgust. He walked back along the catwalk.

"What do you want, you little Indian creep?"

"You'll never find your guns that way," Dale said. He guessed that from wherever he had been hiding the man had watched him diving in the water.

The man stopped a few feet from the dock, his hand on the pistol in the waistband of his pants.

"You'll have to swim for them, like I did," Dale said easily. "Didn't you see me?"

He saw Ross appear on the far side of the pen, saw him step out on the row of drums that pitched and danced under his feet. Don't let this guy turn around, Dale told himself, or he'll see Ross. Keep talking, keep his attention.

"What's the matter, fatso? You can't swim?"

The man swabbed his face with his sleeve and glared at Dale. "Keep your mouth shut, you little punk, or I'll shut it for you!"

Dale held his breath as Ross neared the end of the catwalk. Each step threatened to throw him into the water, but Ross seemed not to notice. Later Dale learned that Ross had been one of the Mohawks who were high-steel workers in New York City, one of the men with bowstring reflexes who helped raise Manhattan's skyscrapers.

Now Ross was on the catwalk, moving as silently as a cloud. Now he was just two paces behind the man.

"Well, fatso, if you can't swim..." Dale said.

Ross snaked his left hand around the man's waist and seized the gun. His right hand landed between the man's shoulders with a powerful shove. The man gave a hoarse shout and flailed his arms as he pitched forward.

"...maybe you better take some lessons," Dale finished as the man hit the water with a resounding splash.

An hour later Barney Watt and Lee were back at the island. With Barney was a Canadian Customs agent. Lee had brought another police officer who was equipped with a face mask, swim fins, and an air tank. He and the agent went out on the catwalks to begin retrieving the contraband firearms.

"We've got a present for you," Dale said to Barney and Lee. He led them to the end of the dock where Ross watched over their catch. Sullen and shivering, the man held on to one of the pilings.

He was very cold and quite uneasy. He had been forced to remain in the water; a paddle across his knuckles had ended his efforts to climb out. His cursing had brought no response; neither of the two Indians had spoken to him. They stood with their backs turned, talking in low tones.

The man brightened when he saw another white man and a man in uniform approaching. "Get me out of here!" he demanded. "I'm freezing!" His anxiety returned when he saw the man in uniform was another Indian.

Lee handcuffed the man before he let him climb out and stand gasping and dripping on the dock. Lee stood behind him, holding his arms firmly.

The man appealed to Barney, the only other white man in sight. "Those Indian bastards made me stay down there in the water!"

But Barney said nothing; he stepped away and left the man facing Ross and Dale. The younger Indian frowned at him; he was holding a paddle which he passed from hand to hand. The older man's face was stern and dark, his hand brushed against a knife in a sheath on his belt.

"You and the other man hurt our people," the older Indian said to him. "You have much to answer for."

Dale reached out and tapped the man on his forehead. The man flinched; the touch could as easily have been a blow. "You will pay for our fish," Dale told him, "and unless you tell this man what he wants to know you will go back in the water."

Ross took a half step closer, forcing the man to look up into his face. "If we put you back in the water," Ross said slowly, "you will have lost your fingernails."

The man's mouth opened and the color drained from his face. He twisted his head to look at Barney. "Did, did you hear that? Did you hear what he said?"

Barney smiled pleasantly. "I didn't hear a thing," he said casually. "Now what about this partner of yours, where did you say we can find him?"

The recovery of the firearms would be completed in another hour or so. The prisoner sat in Lee's boat, tied securely. His accomplice would be in custody by nightfall, thanks to radio.

"Lee, can you finish up here?"

"Sure thing, Barney. Take care."

The agent turned to Dale. "Well, that's the end of your problem here. Let's go back to town."

"Sure." The problem wouldn't be over until he told Rory that the Brown Island Project was ruined, and not before, Dale told himself. He shook hands with Ross and stepped into the boat.

Back at the landing on the reservation Barney said, "How about a late lunch at the Bear's Den? My treat."

Dale realized he was starving. The Bear's Den restaurant in Hogansburg had great food and a three-layer chocolate pie that was superb. "Fine, if we go by the office first."

Patsy met him at the door, her face serious. "Lee called when he was back in town and told me about the damage," she said, "and I got hold of Mr. Horn in Washington." She paused. "I told him what happened."

Dale stared at her. "How'd he take it? Is he mad?"

"He did say some impolite things," Patsy answered, "but he's not really mad. He said to tell you not to worry. The fish farm idea is too good to drop, and we'll start it up again in the spring, bigger and better."

Weak with relief, Dale sagged against the door. "Why, that's great!"

"One other thing." Patsy grinned at him impishly. "You like trout, don't you, Dale?"

"Sure. Why?"

"Mr. Horn wants us to start working on a cookbook."

The Red Oaks

I had just filled the kindling box and brought in the first armload of firewood; familiar rituals that mark the end of autumn. It was late September and we were already having frost; soon there would be snow on the mountains.

The knock on the door was a surprise; I wasn't expecting anybody. I got another surprise when I opened it; I don't get visits from attractive, well-dressed women.

"Mr. Sessions? May I speak to you?" She had striking blue eyes. She was tall, had brown hair, wore tailored slacks instead of jeans, a cashmere sweater. There was the lilt of a French accent. "I'm Louise LaRocque."

"Come in, please." I asked her to be seated, offered coffee. She shook her head, smiling.

"My husband, Paul LaRocque, and I have a camp on Clay Point Road, by Union Lake."

I nodded; I know the area. The term camp usually means a fishing or hunting shack; a camp on Union Lake would be an expensive vacation home.

She got right to the point, her blue eyes fixed on my face. "Somebody has been stealing our timber!"

She waited for a reaction. I said I was sorry or something as lame. Timber piracy happens a lot here in the Adirondacks.

"How much acreage do you have?" I asked.

"I don't know exactly. About twenty acres, including the house. Paul said the trees are hardwood."

"You ought to report the theft to Herb Seymour, the forest ranger in this area."

"Yes, I left a message with his service." The blue eyes were big and serious. "Paul is in Toronto on business, but he told me to ask you if you could help us, Mr. Sessions. Paul knows you used to be in law enforcement."

I'm a retired deputy. People still come to me with problems. I help when I can. "Have you seen anything unusual?" I asked.

She shook her head. "The trees are on a hill behind us. I thought I noticed a gap and walked up there." She paused. "They must have taken over a hundred trees!"

She shook her head and gave me a bit of a smile. "Is there anything you can do?" she asked. "Paul will be happy to pay you."

"Not necessary," I answered. "I'll look into it."

"Thank you." A smile, a handshake, and she was gone. I watched her drive away in a little green Honda. She was composed, self-assured. Late thirties, I told myself. Early forties, tops. Could have been a model.

She had said that Paul told her to do so and so. She didn't look like the kind of woman to be ordered around. Someone had pointed out her husband to me once. He had to be ten years older. Said to have a high post in the government, drove a Volvo, came down on weekends.

I wished Louise LaRocque had stayed for coffee; she would have made good company. I decided against building a fire and went out to the kitchen to feed Clyde, my dog.

Next morning was a beautiful day, crisp and bright, the trees still in color, the sky as blue as—I was surprised at the thought that came to me—as Louise LaRocque's eyes.

I tried to reach Herb Seymour, the ranger, to see if he knew anything about the theft and found out he was out leading the search for a pair of lost hikers. So I started at square one.

Clyde loves to ride in the car; I let him hop in the back of the Bronco and we set out to do some exploring. Stealing a tree is about as hard as stealing a house. Not a little five-foot cedar for the living room at Christmas but a mature tree that's fifty feet high and weighs maybe a ton.

You'll make a lot of noise and you'll take a lot of time. You'll need manpower and heavy equipment and transport. If somebody comes along and asks why you are stealing his house you look blank and say, "Oops, I must have the wrong address." If it's trees, you say, "Sorry, I didn't see the boundary markers," and get ready to run.

But if you don't get caught you sell the trees you've pirated and make a lot of money. If they are choice hardwoods you make a large amount of money.

People have been stealing timber here in upstate New York ever since the early settlers chased the British back into Canada in 1814. Sometimes for firewood, sometimes for lumber to build a barn. Right now with the market so high it's for money, and stealing trees is grand larceny. An oak tree that's worth four hundred dollars standing in the forest can be worth three times that delivered to the mill.

I drove out to Clay Point Road and located the LaRocque place. It was a nice-looking house backed up against a small hill and with a dock at the edge of the water. A small colony of Canadians own homes around the lake; we're less than two hours south of Montreal. And with Whiteface on one side and the Sentinel range on the other you couldn't find a nicer mountain location.

The Union Lake development fizzled out when it became known that acid rain had killed this lake as it has hundreds of small lakes in the Adirondacks. Still the area is busy on weekends; the Canadians entertain each other and go shopping in Plattsburgh or Lake Placid.

The green Honda wasn't in sight. I hoped Louise hadn't gone back up to Canada; I would like to see her again. She had been calm and cool in a situation where other women would have been frantic.

The tree line began below the ridge and swept over the hill. From a tax map I had learned that a conservation outfit called the Nature Trust owned six hundred acres to the south. The Union Lake developer had divided his parcel into parallel strips, each with lake frontage. LaRocque owned the first section, flanked by the Trust on one side and a party named Reeves on the other.

You need a road or at least a trail to get stolen trees out of the woods and there was nothing on this side of the hill. There had to be an access road on the other side.

It was a graveled farm road running through second growth woods and abandoned fields. Soon I found what I was looking for. Someone had placed a ten-inch pipe in the ditch and covered it with fill to make a culvert. Then they brushed out a trail up into the timber.

Beside the road there was a good stack of four-foot pulpwood, a common enough sight since the paper mills have an insatiable appetite for pulp. Obviously the trail had been made to bring the wood out.

There were other items of interest: a truck with the Bird Company's logo on the door, and a Bird employee named Page Brewster. I stopped and got out.

"How you doing, Page?"

"Fine. And you, Hank?"

Anyone could tell Page was a lumberman. He wore the classic wool plaid shirt, jeans, and the hightop boots with steel toes. Page is over fifty and he doesn't have the strength and stamina he once had. Now he does less demanding jobs for his boss, Clayton Bird, like watching over this stack of pulpwood.

"Who you cutting for?" I asked, eyeing the wood.

"Bird's got a deal with old man Reeves."

That meant that Reeves had hired Bird to harvest the pulp off his property; the terms would be a secret between them.

I looked at the new trail leading off into the woods. How far did it go? Had it been used to bring out anything besides small spruce and popple? Pretending to watch Clyde, who was roaming, I took a few steps up the trail. Page moved to stop me.

"Mr. Reeves don't like strangers on his woodlot," he said pleasantly. "You know how it is. Hikers and campers."

Page was right about that. Hikers and campers have been the cause of many blazes and fire is the worst threat of all.

I called Clyde and we headed home, or that's how it looked to Page. Years of police work have taught me how to read people and I could tell there was something Page didn't want me to see. I doubled back almost to the main road, took the Bronco cross-country for a piece and left it on the edge of the timber.

I pushed through a belt of trees and brush and stepped into a sight that was sickening to me. Dozens of stumps where there had been tall, stately oak trees. Piles of limbs. Ferns and sheep laurel broken and trampled. There was a faint smell in the air: crushed leaves, resin bleeding from stumps, dampness from moss that had been in perpetual shadow.

I can't tell a red oak from a white oak. Or from a black oak, for that matter. When I was active I was more interested in keeping marijuana out of schools than learning the fine points of the timber business. But I hate to see trees destroyed for no constructive purpose, just for greed.

A couple of birds circled overhead. A lot of wildlife had been displaced; it would survive but it would take eighty years to see mature trees here again.

I moved around the area until I found a fresh trail leading west down the slope. I didn't have to walk it; I knew it would make a dogleg and connect with the new trail from the lower road.

And parked under some scrub pine I found a skidder. This machine is pure brute strength. It has tires as tall as I am. It has a 'dozer blade in front and a large cable winch in the rear. In between there's a hundred and seventy horsepower. A good skidder man can bull out a trail, pick up four hardwood logs at a time and have a truck loaded before noon.

The skidder was much too big to handle four-foot lengths of pulp. A hoist bolted to the rear of a truck is enough for that. This had to be the machine used to steal Paul LaRocque's timber. It could have been borrowed or stolen. Or it could belong to Clayton Bird.

It was lunch time and I was hungry. I detoured over to Route 9 and stopped at the Noonmark Diner, remembering to get a hamburger, no pickle, for Clyde.

Clayton Bird is around forty, a newcomer to the area. He came over from New Hampshire about five years ago and set up as a logger. Not married, wears his hair long, runs to weight.

He gets a lot of jobs by outbidding everyone else, and the talk is that Bird crews make good money. I had seen Clayton Bird's name somewhere in the past few weeks. Nothing exciting, just something routine. It would come to me. Right now I was going to visit the two lumber mills in our valley.

"Hey there, Smitty."

"Hi, Hank, what's happening?"

Bob Smith and I go back a long ways. I don't think I've ever seen him without a charge of tobacco in his cheek. He's a top scaler at the Rogers and White mill. His job is to grade the logs when they are brought in—prime, select, clear, and so on. Then he checks the size, the shape, and the length, at the same time looking for defects like knots, stains, too big a heart. Finally he calculates the board feet, usually expressed in thousands.

Most mills put out a detailed list of the prices they pay. Bob let me look at his. I saw that hard maple logs eighteen inches in diameter at the small end and classified as prime would bring nine hundred dollars per thousand. Cherry and red oak a couple of hundred more, butternut and yellow birch about half as much.

"How's business these days?" I asked Smitty. It was a casual question; I knew the market was high. Harvesting out West was being hamstrung by regulations; demand for wood from Europe and Asia was driving up the prices everywhere.

"Can't find enough black cherry," Smitty said. "It's scarcer than white ash. You got any in that itty-bitty woodlot of yourn?"

"Nope. Mine's all white pine."

"Make you a good price for it."

"No thanks. I'm saving it for my old age."

That got a laugh. I'm older than Smitty. "Any strangers trying to sell to you these days?" I asked him.

"Nope, just our regulars."

Some mills only buy softwood. Others only buy hardwood. Professional loggers keep in close touch with the mills they sell to, and they only cut what they can sell readily. But with prices going up there's always some amateurs who want to get in the business by poaching timber.

A tempting target is the State of New York, which owns four million acres of timber, most of it here in the Adirondacks. It's impossible to patrol that much. Another target is the absentee owner, like Paul LaRocque.

Thieves try for hardwood trees first because they're worth more. Hardwoods grow almost anywhere but they're more plentiful where certain conditions are most favorable—soil, drainage, elevation. There's a wide belt of choice hardwoods—oak, maple, ash, cherry—that reaches from the Sentinel range north to the Union Lake area and west to Rainbow Lake.

I had a few more words with Smitty and left. Neither mill had been offered any oak logs lately. No surprise there; the stolen trees would have been taken out of the area.

Back on the road again I recalled where I had seen Clayton Bird's name. Over a week ago I dropped by the sheriff's office to pass the time of day. When I'm there I always read the catch-all file: police reports, complaints, gun permits, property transfers, civil actions.

That's where I had seen Bird's name. Two weeks ago he had applied for a passport.

Business must be good, I thought. Travel while you are young enough to enjoy it. I went to Europe once but Uncle Sam controlled the itinerary and there was no time for sight-seeing.

I had been hoping to see Louise LaRocque again, and I did. Her little green sedan was waiting in my driveway as I drove up. She was wearing some sort of jumpsuit which was very flattering. The early sunset behind her made her hair a bronze helmet.

We shook hands and Clyde got his ears scratched by someone who knew how to scratch ears. Her blue eyes fixed on my face, she said, "Paul told me to contact a timber specialist. I gave him your name, Mr. Sessions. I hope you don't mind."

"Call me Hank. I don't mind." Again I suggested coffee.

"I wish I could stay, Hank," she said, "but I can't. Maybe another time?" She gave me the kind of smile your best girl gave you when she said she had saved you the last dance.

I felt very pleased with myself when I went in the house, although I hadn't done anything. It wasn't just the blue eyes and the attention. Meeting this woman was a bright spot in what I admit is a monochromatic life.

My friend Mildred had to spoil the feeling for me. She is a widow; I'm a widower. She has been hinting that we should spend our twilight years together. Mildred does housework for some of the Canadian families, including the LaRocques.

She phoned to tell me that Louise had asked her where I lived. She waited for me to explain why, which

I did as briefly as possible. Without prompting Mildred filled me in on the family.

Louise had been a secretary in a law firm. Instead of going back and forth to Montreal like the other wives, she stayed at the lake all summer. Lonesome, she is," Mildred said. "Only me and her pet tabby cat for company. She is a pretty good cook, I'll give her that. And him, he may be a hero to his stockholders but he's a regular bear at home. Nothing ever suits him.

"Ada Coonrod cleans for the Saint Clairs, and she says when they're at a party Mister LeeRock is a real skirt chaser. Can't keep his hands to hisself. And at his age, too."

I asked, as casually as possible, if the family knew Clayton Bird.

"That one! He came around a month or so ago to deliver some firewood. Took his time about unloading it and got to talking to the missus. Now he drops in every now and then. Seems like a nice enough fella. Sort of stuck on hisself.

"Ada told me the Saint Clair girl is pregnant and her folks are hoppin' mad about it..."

Gossip. I wish the world could get along without it. Mildred made everything sound like a soap opera.

"Paul told me to contact a timber specialist," Louise had told me. It was the logical thing to do—hire an expert to appraise the stolen timber. The man was at my door the next morning. Gilbert Featherstone was a forestry expert registered with the DEC. His testimony would be accepted in court if it came to that.

"Mrs. LaRocque said you might direct me to the area in question," he said pleasantly. He was clean-shaven, middle-aged. He wore a canvas hat and a wool jacket with leather patches on the elbows. He looked more like a college professor than a lumberman.

"I'll be glad to take you there," I said.

I left Clyde on the back porch and we drove out to Union Lake and hiked up the hill. I was looking forward to seeing the forester at work, inspecting the scene of the crime.

As soon as he saw the stumps he said, "Red oak. Very big market for it now." He looked closely at the trees still standing. If they were healthy it was certain the pirated trees had been healthy.

From a satchel Gil produced a camera and took some general views of the area. He had a small sign with his name on it and a slate board on which he chalked the date and a location reference. He made sure these were in every picture.

Then he took close-ups of the saw marks on some of the stumps and the rings in the wood. He had me hold an auxiliary flash to augment the lighting. The marks and rings on the stump can be matched up with those on the butt end of a log, just like fingerprints. That proof will hold up in court, IF you can find the log before it is cut up or shipped away.

Bob Smith had told me a red oak log is usually sliced up into strips of veneer for furniture making, or sometimes the ends are coated with wax and the log is shipped overseas.

While Gil was counting and measuring the stumps, I walked around, looking for anything that would tell us who actually felled the trees. A ragged vee of geese flew high overhead, heading south. I saw a rabbit dart into a pile of limbs, probably looking for new winter quarters.

The skidder was gone. Somebody, maybe Page Brewster, had driven it down the road and loaded it on a flatbed trailer and taken it away. I wondered why anyone would leave a ninety-thousand-dollar machine unattended.

I pointed out the pulpwood operation to Gil and said I thought it had been a cover for pirating the oak trees. He agreed.

"It points at Bird," he said, "but there's no hard proof. Somebody went to Mr. Reeves and made him an offer for his pulpwood he couldn't refuse. That's how he got access to the woodlot here."

An hour later Gil put away his notebook. "I've got the price sheets of all the mills within a hundred miles of here," he told me, "and the mileage bonuses they pay. I'll work out some kind of average based on the top grade for red oak."

He looked around at the stumps again. "He got two logs out of each tree, sometimes three. I'll figure about half were eighteen-inch, and half were fourteen-inch." He glanced at me. "Got to be fair about it, you know."

"Right," I said. "How long do you figure it took to do all this?"

Gil considered the question. "That man Bird or whoever it was obviously had a mill lined up to take delivery before he started. And I'm assuming he could put more than one truck on the road.

"If he was smart he would fell and deliver one load at a time. It's not a good idea to stockpile hardwood; it can dry on you. The better part of three weeks, I'd say."

He closed up his satchel. "Let's stop by a garage. I'll top off your tank."

I started to object. "Not to worry," he said with a grin. "It'll go on the expense account."

I brought Gil back to the house. I don't keep liquor but I do make a good pot of hazelnut coffee. Clyde forgave us for leaving him behind.

Gil told me that sometimes loggers caught poaching are banned from working in certain areas. "Maybe there's a new player in the game here," he said. "I'll look into that."

He took a small white envelope out of his pocket and showed me a hundred-dollar bill inside. He handed the envelope to me. "Hold this for me, Hank. I'm going fishing. If I have any luck I'll call you later."

I learned afterwards that Gil visited the Blue Ax and the Broadway, the local taverns, and spread around a few twenty-dollar bills along with discreet inquiries.

The phone rang after dinner. It was Gil. "Hank, you know a young man named Brice Simpson?"

"I know him."

"He says he can tie the Bird outfit into that timber theft. He'll be over to your house tonight or tomorrow. Listen to what he has to say and then give him that envelope you're holding."

"Wait a sec, Gil. I know Simpson. He'll make a lousy witness."

"I know that. From what I can determine Bird is the logical suspect, but it's all circumstantial. I'll take what I've got to LaRocque. Thanks for your help, Hank."

About ten o'clock there was a knock at the door. Clyde roused himself and barked. It was Brice Simpson.

He is a tall, muscular young man in his middle twenties with a loose-lipped grin and an innocent stare. I chased him off my property once when he wanted to set some apples out as bait during deer season. I doubt if he remembers that.

"How do, Mr. Sessions."

"Come on in, Brice."

"Man down at the Ax said you might be holding something for me. Said that I was to tell you what I seen." He looked at me expectantly.

"What was that, Brice?"

"I seen some of the Bird crew loading up them oak logs."

"You see Mr. Bird himself?"

"No, sir. Only Tony and that feller they call Red."

"When was this?"

"'Bout ten days ago or maybe twelve."

I knew Brice Simpson would have little or no credibility as a witness, but I felt that Gil Featherstone knew what he was doing. I handed Brice the envelope. He opened it and his eyes widened as he saw the bill inside.

"Hello, Mr. Pres-i-dint," he said.

Carefully he folded the envelope and placed it in his pocket. I held the door open for him as he went out.

"One thing, Brice," I said.

"What's that, Mr. Sessions?"

"You ought to put some of that down on your child support payments."

By the stricken look on his face I knew the thought would have never occurred to him.

"Yes, sir. I'll think on it."

After Brice had gone I left the porch light on for a while. It had started to snow and I stood there watching it. The first snow is the pretty one.

Two weeks and three inches of snow later Paul LaRocque filed suit against Clayton Bird. The law says a victim of timber piracy can sue for treble damages and that's what LaRocque's lawyers did.

They showed that the property had been duly surveyed and the boundaries marked. They presented Gil Featherstone's credentials as a forestry expert. They asked for $540,000, three times Gil's estimate of the fair market value. They spelled out willful trespass, damage to the trees left standing, damage to the aesthetic appearance of the property, damage to its future value.

The problem was proof. There were no witnesses against Bird himself. None of the pirated red oak logs had been found, here in the States or in Canada. The suit could take months and there was a good chance that the court would award LaRocque only the value of the trees as they stood in the forest. That would be about a third of what Bird would have collected when he sold the logs. Some timber thieves would settle for that kind of profit.

The next day Clayton Bird filed a petition for bankruptcy. This gave him protection against any over-anxious creditors, and confused anyone who thought he had actually stolen and sold a great deal of choice hardwood.

I was amazed at how fast Bird managed this. He must have had the paperwork all done in advance. And that answered my question about the skidder. If he wasn't going to use it any longer or if the bank was going to repossess it, it didn't make much difference where it was parked.

That same day I happened to be passing Sloane's Likker Locker and saw Louise's little Honda parked out front. I saw her inside buying two bottles of champagne. Ted Sloane gave her change and put the bottles in a bag.

I held the door open for her when she came out. It was a cold day and there was color in her cheeks. Her blue eyes sparkled as she greeted me.

"Having a celebration?" I asked. She stared at me and her face turned white. "What do you mean?" she asked in a weak voice. For an instant she seemed alarmed, almost frightened of me or what I had said.

"Champagne usually means a celebration," I said quickly. "Your anniversary?"

She took a deep breath and managed a smile. "No, Hank, just a little birthday party."

"Have a nice time," I said, feeling foolish. I held the door of her car open for her and brushed some drifted snow off the windshield. She put her package on the seat and reached out to shake hands.

"Thank you, Hank," she whispered. "Have a nice winter."

"You, too, Louise."

She drove away and I stood there on the slushy sidewalk. I hadn't meant to be nosy about the champagne. It was none of my business.

I didn't sleep very well. I kept thinking about all those trees destroyed for no reason other than greed. Next morning I decided to visit my secret isolation spot.

This is a place up on Haystack where I used to go when the world began stepping on my heels. It's on the east face of the mountain almost at the top where the trail turns back down.

There's an outcropping of granite and a flat place you can sit. Here's the secret: if you sit here and look straight ahead you will not see a single solitary shred of the existence of mankind.

No trace at all. No roads, no power lines, no fields, no fences, nothing. Just forest and hills and a river, the same as the Algonquins saw, and whoever was here before them.

Of course if a jet crosses the sky you're back in the twentieth century again. And then there are shoes on your feet and the air you are breathing holds whatever it is that causes acid rain, but you don't have to think about those things. You can sit there and look at a pristine world and not be reminded of man and his good works.

I wondered if Louise LaRocque would appreciate my isolation spot the same way I did. Then I stood up to leave; I was acting like an old fool.

A pair of hawks drifted across the sky and spiraled down toward the top of a tree where they must have a nest. That made me think of golden eagles; they are back in these mountains again.

And that made me think of the Nature Trust, Paul LaRocque's neighbor. That outfit does everything it can to protect the forests and the wildlife. Last year it raised Cain with the Air National Guard for flying too low and disturbing the nesting birds. That may sound trivial but now the jets are forbidden to fly lower than two thousand feet.

If the Nature Trust is so solicitous about everything in its part of the forest it would be mighty curious about any timber harvesting going on next door on the LaRocque property. They wouldn't hesitate to ask a lot of questions.

Clayton Bird must have been ready with a mighty good answer when he was stealing those trees. An answer someone had given him.

The fire was going nicely and I was studying the television guide when two phone calls had me on my feet and reaching for my coat and hat.

The first one was from Ed Stewart, a bartender at the Blue Ax. Years ago I had persuaded his son to join the army instead of waiting to be locked up for auto theft. Ed still counts that a favor.

"Thought you would like to know. The Bird crews are in here. Bird gave them a bonus of a week's pay. Said he was going out West hunting."

"Thanks, Ed."

The second call, two minutes later, was from Mildred. "Go to bingo with me tomorrer night, Hank; I'm on a lucky streak! This afternoon Miz LaRocque was all packed to leave and she gave me a present. She gave me that old tabby cat of hern. She gave me fifty dollars toward its keep and made me promise to take good care of it. I'll hit that bingo for sure tomorrer..."

"See you there, Mildred. I've got to go."

I remembered to close the damper on the fireplace before I jumped in the Bronco and left.

Of course Louise didn't take her pet cat back home to Montreal because she wasn't going back to Montreal. And that was a farewell bonus Bird gave his men because he was going to try out his new passport.

I had a hunch they were going to disappear together. Where? Louise wasn't the type to live in Mexico. Canada was her husband's territory. France would make a good starting point for a new life with all that money. And she even spoke the language.

Louise had planned the whole thing. She protected Bird with a forged standing timber sales contract. She researched the market, banked the money, handled the Chapter Eleven paperwork. All of it. And toasted their success with champagne.

She even recruited me to be her champion if she needed one, and all it took was one lovely smile.

What would Clayton do in France? Whatever he was told. He would share in the money of course. I didn't want to think what other incentives she may have offered him.

As a retirement present the county had a telephone installed in my car. I don't use it much but tonight I was very glad to have it. As I headed up Interstate 87 I talked to a contact I have on the Montreal police force. I asked him to use his computer to access some airline passenger lists for transatlantic flights.

I got to Mirabel Airport in time, and my hunch was right. I was sitting in the Air France boarding lounge when they came to the departure gate. Louise was stunning in a navy blue suit and a tiny hat. Clayton was more casual in grey slacks and a charcoal blazer.

I started to wave but thought better of it. It would just be an old man showing off how smart he was. And I'm not in the business of arresting people anymore.

They walked past me and I stood up to leave. Then Louise glanced around and saw me. She stopped and let Clayton walk on ahead. She turned and gave me a smile, a radiant, victorious smile. I could see her lips say the words.

"Goodbye, Hank."

"Good luck, Louise," I whispered.

Then they were gone and I started the long walk to the parking lot. Maybe I should have phoned Paul LaRocque and told him his red oaks had bought a new life for someone he used to know. But I felt sure he would find a note somewhere.

The lonely housewife had seen a fortune in the trees up there on the hill and she reached out and took it. She fooled a lot of people, me included. Now she was gone, but I would remember her smile.

It would be another long winter, but I had plenty of firewood and kindling.

A Pure Kind
of Life

*We promised you 12 mysteries, and this 13th tale gives
you a baker's dozen. While it is not strictly a mystery
story, events in* A Pure Kind of Life *involve two of
the major concerns of Adirondack residents: the environment and a poor economy. Although the happen-
ings are fictitious, they are based on real conditions.
There are now more than three dozen moose living in
the high mountains of the Adirondacks. And due to
unemployment, most North Country towns would be
delighted to be considered as the site of a new prison.*

Foreword

The poacher crouched by the trunk of the tree and
fingered the switch of his lantern. He had picked a
night with an almost full moon and a steady, gentle
breeze that blew from behind him across a small open
space in the woods.

He had brought his son with him. Tonight was to be a milestone of young manhood for the boy, his first killing of a wild animal. But his son had shown no relish for the hunt, and now he had fallen asleep again.

The poacher yanked at the boy's arm. "Stay awake, Leon," he hissed. "Keep your eyes on that open spot there."

"Ain't no deer coming tonight, Paw," his son whispered sullenly. "Let's go home."

"Shut up. Time a boy your age learned how to jack a deer. Now watch where we put them apples."

The clearing was bright with moonlight. On the ground in its center was a pile of apples, saved from last fall to use as bait. A salt block would have been better but apples were easier to come by.

The scent of the fruit was strong, enticing. A doe, roused from sleep to drink, had caught the inviting smell and followed it. Now she stood on the other side of the clearing, her head turning from side to side.

The breeze denied her the smell of the man and the boy; she stepped out into the moonlight. Her nose outstretched, she reached the pile of apples and halted. A blinding beam of light stabbed her. Facing it, she froze motionless, her head thrown up exposing her neck.

There was a loud crack and a bullet tore though the base of her throat and shattered her right shoulder. The doe fell backward and thrashed convulsively on the ground.

The boy started to his feet. "Jesus, Paw!"

The man put his hand on his son's arm. "Don't go near it, son. Them feet will open you up if they hit you. We'll wait a bit."

The doe made a thin, shrill sound, laden with pain.

"Then kill it now, Paw!"

"Best not to fire another shot, Leon. People hear one shot at night, they think they might be mistook. But they hear another one, they know somebody's jackin'. That deer's hit good; she won't take too long to die."

The wood was full of the noise of the animal's pain. The doe tried repeatedly to stand but could not. At last she fell on her side, shuddering, and lay still in the bloody mud.

"What's the matter with you, boy? Iffen you're goin' to throw up go behind a tree!"

Later the man and the boy walked down an old logging trail to where the truck was concealed. The man carried the body of the deer wrapped in a plastic shower curtain. The boy walked behind, carrying the battery lantern and the rifle.

The man was angry because his son had shamed him. He had told the boy to cut the animal's throat but the boy had mutely refused. The man had cursed and commanded but the boy would not take the knife, and the initiation ritual had gone unserved.

The silence of the night was scornful and mocking. The woods were a cemetery filled with the ghosts of the slain creatures watching him, wishing him out of their company. The man wanted to hurry but his load was heavy. The shower curtain was taped well but he could smell the blood and feel the warmth of the doe's body on his neck and shoulders.

From behind them came a rasping, rumbling sound, and he felt the earth shake beneath his feet. He turned awkwardly and looked down the trail. In the moonlight he saw a monstrous black shape looming just yards from him. A gigantic head stretched toward them, two huge claw-shaped hands reached high in the air, poised to drop down on him and crush him.

The boy whimpered in terror.

The earth shook and the black shape towered higher over them and there was an unearthly, angry snorting noise. The man panicked.

"Run, boy! Run!"

* * * *

"You're going to lose this election, Washington Gladd, if you don't get your head out of that radio!"

Wash nodded but said nothing.

"There'll be enough time for your animals next month, Wash. You better get downtown today and let some people see you."

Into the microphone Wash said, "Got to go, Dale. Talk to you later." He took off the headset and turned to face his wife standing in the doorway of his little room off the kitchen. She was right, he thought, and he could come back to the radio this afternoon while she was at work at the hospital.

"Another cup of coffee first?" he asked.

"All right," Nora said. "But get a move on."

They sat at the table in the big kitchen of their small house. Nora was ten years younger than Wash, but the alchemy of marriage had made them draw close in appearance; both greying, thin, sharp-eyed mountain people. Nora would retire in two years and they would take interesting trips but now Wash had an election to win.

It was still early in the morning; daybreak usually found activity in their kitchen. Outside the window the maples showed September color. Overhead the sky was a brilliant blue and in the distance Whiteface was a slate giant thrusting against it. Doc, the old collie, thumped his tail at their voices but did not stir from his box by the stove. The Gladd place had sheltered dozens of animals that were lost, injured or abandoned; Doc was the first and had stayed on after the others had gone to new homes.

Wash stirred sugar into his coffee. "You know I don't care if I'm elected councilman or not," he said to his cup, not wanting to look at his wife.

"The town needs you, Wash," Nora said stubbornly. "Almost everybody says so."

This was an often repeated exchange, with no feeling left in it. Wash would do what Nora wanted him to do, and it was her idea for him to run for councilman. It was part of her campaign to get him to slow down, to spend less time roaming the woods, fretting about the wildlife.

Take Wash out of the woods, Dr. Kay had said, and you might as well put him in a pine box. But she would try. Wash was past sixty-five, still erect, still lean, but Nora knew the shortness of breath, the aches and pains that plagued him. As councilman he would have to spend more of his time in town, maybe all of it.

"Now today, Wash," she said briskly, "you've got to get out and talk to people. I hear Barney Freeman is in town most every day, shaking hands and blowing off."

"Most everybody in town knows me, Nora," he said mildly. "I drove that mail truck for twenty-two years." He grinned at her. "And I had my picture in the paper which is more than Barney Freeman ever did."

Nora reached behind her and took a scrapbook from a shelf on the wall and opened it to the page with the newspaper article. She looked at it proudly. "Yes, you sure did that," she said.

The picture was of Wash, hatless, standing next to a man in a ranger hat in front of a wooden tower on a rocky ledge and holding a small covered box. The caption read:

LOCAL MAN WELCOMES
EAGLES TO NEW HOME

Shown with NYS Department of Environmental Conservation spokesman Edgar Frost is Mr. Washington Gladd, of Monroe, prominent conservationist. They are installing eighteen baby bald eagles from Alaska atop Whiteface Mountain as a part of a 12-year program by the DEC to restore breeding populations of endangered species to New York. Mr. Gladd, an active conservationist, was instrumental in introducing petting zoos at tourist information centers along the Northway, and has been campaigning for a county-wide leash law to protect the increasing deer population from roving bands of domestic dogs.

"That was over three months ago," Nora said, "and you'd be surprised how fast people forget."

"Yes, chief," Wash said, "I'm going into town right after you leave."

Nora knew she had his promise and she changed the subject. "What did Dale have to say on the radio this morning?"

Wash brightened. "Dale says Number Two is getting restless. I wish I could see him, Nora. The first moose in the Adirondacks for over two hundred years, and now there's one right here in Clinton County. I bet he's a beauty! I'll call Dale again this afternoon."

"Now, Wash, Dr. Porter has plenty of people there at Huntington to help him keep track of that animal. He doesn't need you pestering him on the radio every few hours."

"I know."

She reached over and put her hand on his shoulder. "We've got about enough saved for that trip to Alaska. We'll see plenty of animals up there, Wash."

Nora stood up. "I'm late, I have to go. Remember now, I switched shifts with Connie at the hospital so I can meet you at the town hall at six for that public meeting about the prison."

"All right. I'll do the dishes."

"And when you go take some of those posters with you. You know Barney's been taking them down behind your back."

Wash did the breakfast dishes and left them to drain. The scrapbook still lay on the table. He riffled through the pages of commendations and letters of appreciation from civic groups and wildlife organizations, then he closed the book and put it back on the shelf.

He picked up his hat and started out the back door, then returned and got a dozen of the campaign posters their daughter Ellie had made up for him. They were small sheets of white cardboard with precise lettering in red and blue. Wash didn't care much for the message, but Nora and Ellie were proud of it.

VOTE FOR WASHINGTON
YOU'LL BE GLADD YOU DID!!

He put the posters on the back seat of his jeep and drove the three miles into town. For most of the way the road followed the river. The stream was low at this time of year, and sumac made red streaks along the banks. Be snow on Whiteface any day now, he thought. Deer will be coming down from the high places.

Moose Number Two stood at the edge of a meadow and looked at the herd of dairy cows grazing peacefully below him. Weeks ago the cows had been alarmed when he had appeared among them but now they accepted his presence at the edge of their pasture. Number Two lowered his huge head and snuffled at the grass without interest.

Around his neck was a wide leather strap which held a small but powerful radio transmitter. Number Two had forgotten the strap was there; he did not remember the day months ago when a steel dart had stung his side and he had slowly gone down on his knees and rested his big scoop-shaped antlers on the ground.

A team of men had taken a sample of his blood, examined his teeth, and given him an injection of antibiotics. When he got to his feet the men were gone and there was a small tag in each ear and the strap with its radio was around his neck.

Over a year ago Number Two and three other moose, all bulls, had wandered down from Canada into the Adirondack Mountains. Perhaps they were searching for mates or were tired of their home prairies. But ahead of them there had always been a fresh stand of maples or an interesting scent or a good spot for shelter, so they had continued on their way.

Eventually they had separated and roamed the mountains alone. They were quiet, solitary animals, and their mammoth size protected them from predators. But they had been seen by humans and reported because no moose had lived in the Adirondacks for two hundred years.

News of the sightings reached the Adirondack Wildlife Program and students from the Environmental Science and Forestry department of the SUNY College in Newcomb had searched them out, and had tracked them for over a year.

Today, as he had been yesterday and the day before, Number Two was restless. He had walked completely around the meadow several times, stopping to scratch the remaining velvet from his antlers against the branches of trees.

The forage here was good, the water was good, but some instinct was suggesting that he move on. It was not a conscious decision; Number Two merely turned his head away from the meadow, chose a path between trees large enough to permit passage of his huge rack, and walked away.

Outside of town, Wash drove past a large field that was filled with junked cars, rusting like boulders in a sea of weeds. If I am elected, Wash thought, maybe I can get the town to do something about this eyesore.

When Wash was a young boy this highway had been busy from morning to night with logging trucks. Before that it had carried giant wagons creaking with the weight of iron ore. Today what little traffic there was consisted of local people, venturesome tourists, travelers who had strayed off the Northway that ran from Montreal to Albany. Fifty miles away Lake Placid was an oasis of wealth and activity but Monroe, like so many other small mountain towns, was an empty shell.

Barney Freeman and some other men thought a new prison was the answer to the town's problems.

Highway 374 became the main street of Monroe for a few blocks and continued on its way east to Dannemora. Wash turned into the parking lot of the Grand Union. The lot held a few economy cars and some pickup trucks; the people of Monroe did not drive station wagons or Cherokees or Blazers.

He took a poster from the back seat and went into the bank. One of the tellers saw him come in and waved. His poster was gone from the community bulletin board; Wash replaced it and went over to say hello.

"How're the babies doing, Wash?"

"Real good, Evelyn. We think they'll winter just fine."

Evelyn shook her head. "And you flew those little eagles all the way down from Alaska."

Wash smiled. "I didn't. The DEC went and got them and United flew them down, for free."

He would have stayed longer but a customer walked up and Wash turned away. "Way to go, Wash!" Evelyn called after him. He would have to remember to tell Nora that not everybody had forgotten about the bald eagles.

Down the street at Bob's Barber Shop there was the usual morning crowd sitting across the room from Bob's barber chair. There was a rack of tattered magazines for children to look at on Saturdays, and several pairs of snowshoes crossed on the walls. This was the unofficial headquarters for the volunteer fire department; a CB radio sat on a shelf next to a big coffee maker and a pile of cups.

"Morning, Wash."

"Gentlemen."

Wash saw that his poster was still in place but he couldn't just turn around and leave; he would have to stay and talk for a few minutes. There was one empty chair but he stood by the door. He knew Bob liked to keep at least one chair open for customers.

Ned Sourwine waved at him from his usual place in the chair by the window. Ned wasn't too bright but he was harmless and he was tolerated because he was from the town's oldest family.

"You see what Barney Freeman's got to say there, Wash?" Ned said.

Wash turned and looked at Barney's poster as if he had never seen it before. "LOCK UP YOUR FUTURE WITH BARNEY FREEMAN," he read aloud.

"He's talkin' about the new prison he wants to bring in here if we'll all get behind it," Ned went on in a loud, high voice. "All we have to do is to ask for it. Lyon Mountain down here's got one, Altona's got one, Chateaugay's got one, Moriah's got one, Malone's got two, and Paul Smith's got one." Ned sat forward, staring at Wash. "Barney says we can get us one, easy."

Behind his chair Bob stopped working his scissors on his customer's head. Bob didn't like Ned, didn't like him coming into his shop every day, taking the best customer chair, only getting his hair cut twice a year. He usually didn't speak to Ned at all, but today Bob was irritated. He put down his scissors and turned around.

"It's not that simple, Ned," Bob said. "You got to have a site the state approves of, you got to have water to it, you got to have sewer, and transportation, and God knows what all. Don't you know about that, Ned?"

"That's right, Ned," Wash said gently. "You think we can handle all that?" The other men in the shop were listening; the town would vote on the prison issue at tonight's meeting. Everybody knew that Wash didn't much like the idea.

Ned was flattered at the attention he was receiving. He frowned and tried to look wise. "Prison would mean lots of jobs," he said. "Even a little prison like the one Paul Smith's got." He cackled suddenly. "I sure could use some of that prison money."

Bob pointed his scissors at Ned. "You going to work there, Ned?" Bob pretended to be surprised. "I didn't know you was Civil Service. Man's got to be Civil Service to work prison."

Bob enjoyed the crestfallen look on Ned's face, and went on. "Or maybe you planning to help build it, Ned?" Bob shook his head in mock regret. "That won't work, neither, Ned. Contractor comes in here to build the prison, he brings his own crew. The prison goes up and the men leave here and the money goes with them. Now where does that leave you, Ned?"

The men grinned at each other and looked at Ned, who was now slouched down in his chair. Wash didn't much like Ned, but for different reasons. Ned let his dogs roam freely through the woods; this winter it would be Sourwine dogs that chased and crippled deer.

"Here's what you do, Ned," Wash said to him, "you hire on in the prison barber shop."

"I can't give no haircuts," Ned answered sullenly.

"Sure you can, Ned," said Wash. "You've sat here and watched enough of them."

The men laughed and Wash went back out on the sidewalk.

"Number Two is moving," said a man at a radio set miles away. "He's been headed northeast for an hour."

"Watch him, Tom." A second man looked closely at a map that had three red pins stuck into it. "If he doesn't turn back or change direction we'll let Wash Gladd know he's moving his way."

He walked into another room where a man was seated at a desk with three telephones on it. "One of the big boys is moving," he said. "Be sure somebody's on the hot line round the clock. You know the drill, Ray. Anybody sees him, stay away from him. Moose are dangerous anytime, worse now that fall is coming."

Another poster was missing from the window of the National Bell Store; Barney was making a game of taking them down. Wash went inside to replace it. The big store was empty except for Helen Coonrod at her cash register by the door. Helen and Wash had gone to high school together.

"What do you think about the prison idea, Wash?"

Wash looked around the store, at the pipe racks of work clothes and blue jeans and wool shirts. Each rack carried a large SALE! sign.

"Probably good for business, Helen," he said.

She nodded. "It would be that, all right. But I don't like the idea of convicts right outside of town."

"I don't think you'd have to worry about that, Helen. I'm sure the security would be pretty tight."

Helen shook her head. "I don't mean the prisoners getting away and running around the mountains. I mean the families and friends and people who would be coming in to visit them. Chances are they'd be no better than the men they came to see." Helen smiled, but her eyes were serious when she looked at Wash.

"That's something to think about, Helen, but I don't think they've had any trouble like that over in Malone."

"Well, what about it, Wash? Barney says a prison would be the pot of gold for our town. What do you think?"

Wash sighed. Helen might be another person who thought he was against any kind of progress.

"It might be a good thing for our town, Helen, but what are all these prisons doing to the mountains? Most of the small towns up here live on the tourists and the fishermen and are they still going to come up here when we've got a prison in every town?"

He stopped. He knew that very few tourists ever came into Helen's store; she made a meager living from her local trade.

"I just wish we could get some kind of a factory," he said lamely. In a few minutes he went back out on the sidewalk.

When he walked into the Mountain Sport Shop a bell jingled over the door. The sound brought Buster Farvro out of the back room. The big smile Buster put on for customers faded when he saw Wash. To Buster, Wash was an old busybody, always telling people to keep their dogs penned up and to build more bird houses.

"Morning, Buster," said Wash.

"Morning, Wash."

Buster dressed the way tourists expected from a real outdoorsman; even in summer he wore a checked wool shirt and heavy pants and hunting boots and a big sheath knife on his belt. He was a young man with a shiny black beard and long hair.

Wash knew that Buster took deer out of season, as a lot of local men did, and he had heard that Buster had a little private business on the side. Buster would take a tourist out into the woods and set him up an easy rifle shot at a deer in a spot he had baited. It was something for the tourist to brag about when he got home and extra money in Buster's pocket. Wash didn't know if the story was true; Buster had never been caught.

"Mind if I put this poster on your wall?"

"Go ahead. Iffen you can find room."

The bulletin board was crowded with pictures of game kills by Buster or his friends. Barney Freeman's poster was tacked up but there was no room for Wash's sign. He stuck it on the bottom of the frame and hoped the wind from the door wouldn't blow it off onto the floor.

Wash looked around the small store. With fall coming Buster had put away his displays of fishing tackle and loaded the shop with hunting gear, predominantly archery supplies. Hunting bows hung on the walls, practice targets lined the floor, display cases held boxes of broadhead arrow points. There were packages of various scents which promised to lure a deer to a hunter's stand, and other scents to disguise the human smell.

Wash looked at a small display card in one of the cases. SAVE BIG REPAIR BILLS, the card said, DRIVE WITH DEER ALERT. The card was full of small metal cylinders.

"Those deer horns not moving so good?" Wash asked.

"Naw," said Buster sourly. "Only sold three so far."

Wash insisted that Buster stock the device. Every fall there were many accidents at night in which a car would strike a deer on the road. The deer, transfixed by the car's headlights, would not leap to safety, and the car would be severely damaged, the occupants injured, and the deer often killed.

The deer horn was mounted on the hood or fender of a car. The forward motion created a whistle that was inaudible to humans but could alarm a deer grazing on the side of the road. There would be more deer in the woods this fall, and more accidents.

Wash had canvassed all the salesmen working the area and most of them had put deer horns on their cars. But he didn't have much success with visitors to the area and local people.

"Those horns don't move any better, I'll need that room for something else," Buster said.

"Give them a few more weeks, Buster," Wash said. "I told you I'll take them off your hands if they don't sell."

On top of the display case was a card of broadhead arrow points, sharp thin steel blades ground to razor sharpness. Buster saw Wash look at them. "When are you going to take up bow hunting, Wash?" he asked, grinning.

Wash shook his head. He felt a small surge in his stomach as he thought of a deer plunging frantically through the bush goaded by one of these steel lances. An arrow rarely killed instantly, except for a heart penetration.

"I think a bullet's cleaner," he said mildly.

Buster grinned at the look on the older man's face. Soft-hearted old bastard, he thought. Who does he think he is? Just because he got his picture in the paper.

"Let me show you something new, Wash. Just come in last week."

Buster handed Wash a new hunting arrow. The shaft was metal, the end had the standard configuration of plastic feathers, but the head was different. Instead of the usual two vanes swept back from the point, this broadhead had four vanes, scalpel sharp, over five inches in length.

Buster touched one of the vanes lovingly. "Extra sharp, and there's four of them, see? Your ordinary broadhead has just two blades, and two won't work around inside the deer like these four will.

"Any kind of hit at all and this head is right inside that sucker. Neck, shoulder, chest, leg—these blades will work right in. And with every jump that bastard makes they're cutting him up, muscles, meat, tendons, whatever.

"He's jumping all right, because he's hurting something fierce, and with every jump he'll be slicing himself into hamburger! Yes, sir, with one of these you can hit that sucker anywhere—you don't have to hit the lungs or the heart—and you've got meat on the table!"

Buster paid no attention to the frozen look on Wash's face as he put the arrow back in its rack on the counter. "Well, what do you think, Wash? This baby comes in all standard lengths and it's a damn good buy at eighteen fifty."

Wash felt dizzy and there was a dull pain in his chest. Slowly he walked over to the bulletin board and yanked his poster down and held it tightly in his hand.

"I think it would take a real son of a bitch to use a thing like that on a deer," he said. The bell jingled again as he walked out and closed the door behind him.

Moose Number Two moved steadily through the woods. He stopped at frequent intervals to graze on the leaves of maple and balsam; he would consume sixty pounds of food each day.

He gave no thought to where he was going; having begun to move he was content to remain in motion. He traveled in a straight line, detouring when the trees were too thick to permit passage of his rack of antlers.

Once a wooden fence barred his way. He shouldered through it without effort. For a short while he walked along a road, almost trotting since there were no overhanging branches to catch at his rack and slow his progress. But the road held faint smells that were disturbing and he left it and resumed his march through the second-growth pines and hardwood.

The man at the radio said, "Number Two is still moving. Heading northeast. Has been all morning."

He and the second man looked at the large map. "He's been here in the Chateaugay area for weeks. Maybe he's going to join up with Number One up there north of Miner Lake."

"No, I doubt it," said the second man. "Moose don't pair up. They're loners. Where's Number Three?"

The first man indicated a pin on the map. "Up there by Ellenburg. Been there a long time. Maybe he thinks he's found a girlfriend in a dairy herd up there."

The second man smiled. "Not much chance. I wish he could, though. There hasn't been a moose cow in the Adirondacks for a couple of hundred years."

At the hardware store Wash met Abe Tobin, the manager, checking a freight delivery on the sidewalk. Abe looked at Wash's face and said, "Come on in and set down for a minute. You look terrible."

They sat down and Wash began breathing more easily. He thumped his chest to show Abe what the trouble was. "It catches me like that sometimes," he said. Old friends, they sat in silence.

Finally Abe said, "They giving you a hard time about being against the prison?"

"Who said I was against it?"

"I know you, Wash. You don't see turning these mountains into some sort of penal colony."

"No, sir! Old Wash wants us all to just live in the past!" It was Barney Freeman. He had come in the door and was standing behind them.

"Morning, Barney," said Abe.

"Morning," said Wash.

Wash always thought of a woodchuck when he looked at Barney, a senior member of a superior class of chucks. Barney was stout and had a round face with heavy grey sideburns that widened his face still more. He wore heavy gold-rimmed glasses over guileless blue eyes.

"Morning, Abe. Wash."

Barney took a chair without being invited to. A man and his wife came in, nodded to Abe, and went to the paint counter in the rear. Abe's daughter would take care of them.

Abe sat back in his chair and waited for the argument to start between these two friends of his. As usual, Barney opened the debate.

"Well, Wash, how come you're so set against asking for a prison here in Monroel? Think it would be bad for the town?"

"Not bad for the town, Barney," Wash said slowly. "Bad for the mountains."

The man and his wife were still at the counter. Another man had come into the store and stood behind them. Wash knew they were all listening and would repeat what he and Barney said to each other. There was an ache in his chest, and he wished he was home, or at least had a cup of coffee. But he wanted to make these people, everybody in town, think about the prison question before they jumped on Barney's bandwagon.

"It's another step in the wrong direction. Look what we had right here in Clinton County a hundred years ago. Iron. Mountains full of iron ore. Now it's all gone. And timber, forests of prime hardwood. Now that's gone, too—logged out like there was no tomorrow.

"All we got left is the mountains, clean air, and fishing and lakes and river and nature. Nature is the only resource we've got left. There's millions of people living all around the Adirondacks in the cities, and nature is what brings them up here, to see and enjoy."

Barney was smiling, rolling a pencil in his fingers, waiting for Wash to stop so he could have his say. Wash kept on stubbornly. His words sounded hollow and tired to him because he had said them so often.

"We're a state park, bigger than the whole of Vermont. We could be a national park, like Yellowstone. Keep things the way they are, for people all over to enjoy."

"Can I say something?" Barney asked politely.

"Go ahead."

"What are the two main problems in the northern counties of New York today?" Barney asked judiciously.

Wash knew if he didn't answer one of the other men would chime in.

"Unemployment and drug and alcohol abuse," he said.

"Right. Now wouldn't a source of income help a little town like this one?"

"Sure. But a small industry would be better than a prison. Tourists don't want to come to an area with a lot of prisons."

Barney ignored that. "Wash," he said patiently, "we can't get an industry or factories here because we don't have the weather and the roads, but we could get a prison if we work at it. You just can't think about the wildlife and nature and forget about the people. We can sit here and starve to death or we can try to help ourselves."

"We want our own jobs, not a prison run by the state," Wash said lamely.

224

Barney pretended to be surprised. "You mean the people who work in this here prison won't come in here to Abe's store and buy anything?"

"Sure they will. But do you think the fishermen are going to rent Henry Coonrod's cabins if there's a state prison in the backyard? And how many gas stations are left down there in Gabriel now that the prison's there?"

The debate went on and the audience listened very thoughtfully. But Barney, with his promises of money and stability, seemed a winner.

Wash and Abe had lunch at Gus's Diner, sitting at a table in the rear of the small restaurant. It was noon but there were just three truckers at the counter and no other tables were occupied.

"I've seen this place a lot busier than this," Abe offered. "Maybe we could use that prison, Wash."

"Yes," Wash said. "The town is dying off."

Abe was surprised. "You mean you agree with Barney?"

Wash shrugged. "Town needs something, that's for sure. And prisons have helped other towns around here. Maybe not a whole lot, but some."

"Then why were you arguing with Barney?"

"I want people to think about this a whole lot more before they send that petition to the corrections department," Wash said. "And I'll tell you something, Abe. So does Barney."

He leaned across the table toward his friend. "Look, Abe, maybe we could work out something with the corrections department. We work with them on the land for the prison and they help us to get the DEC to set out the Blue Crane Pond District as a wilderness complex, like down there at Pharaoh Lake."

Abe nodded slowly. "I should have known you'd have something like that up your sleeve. You've wanted that complex for years, haven't you, Wash?"

"A lot of us have. Just look at it, Abe. Maybe we get the prison, but maybe we also can get Blue Crane Pond for the birds and the animals. We could build foot trails through it for the tourists, and it could have its own game warden and the birds could be protected and there would be no more poaching or trapping the beavers..."

He stopped because Abe was grinning at him. "You're always looking out for the animals, aren't you, Wash."

"Somebody's got to," Wash said quietly. Abe was eating french fries with his fingers. Wash wasn't hungry; his stomach felt queasy. He drank his coffee. It was important to him that Abe understood how he felt about the wildlife in the mountains. Wash put down his cup.

"Animals are different, Abe. They don't lie to each other. They don't cheat or steal or try to cross each other up. Abe, animals are the one kind of life that stayed the way God made it and wanted it to be. They are what they are and they're content to stay that way."

He saw Abe smiling at him but he also saw comprehension in his eyes. "I see what you're driving at," Abe said. "Animals can't talk; they can't have money and politics and welfare like we can. That what you mean?"

Wash smiled back at him. "That's it. Animals live a really pure kind of life, and that's the beauty of it."

"This is Dale, Wash. Number Two is moving and he's heading in your direction."

"When did he start?"

"Early this morning."

"Anybody see him yet?"

"No. No calls on the hot line. Tom and Bert are tracking him."

No matter what he was doing Wash was supposed to take a nap after lunch. Today he thought he actually would and not have to fib about it to Nora; the morning had been hard on him. But when he walked in his little study he saw the blinking light on his radio that meant someone at Huntington was trying to reach him.

"There aren't any dairy farms along the route he's taking," Dale said, "so we won't have any herd owners raising hell with us."

"That's good." Whenever one of the moose had roamed into a dairy farm Dale and his researchers had received angry complaints that the moose had upset their cows and interfered with their milk production.

"He's traveling pretty fast," Dale said. "He went around that big tree farm east of Bradley Pond; the growth is too heavy for him to get through it. I think he's following the power lines because it's easier traveling."

"Damn," Wash said. "He'll be an easy target."

"Right. Out in the open like that."

Wash and Dale and the rest of the staff lived with the fear that some clown would see one of the moose and take a rifle and try to kill it. The penalty was a two thousand dollar fine and a year in jail, but that wouldn't stop some people.

"You busy over there, Wash?" Dale asked. "Can you help us on this one?"

"Never too busy," said Wash. "Shoot."

"I'm sending you a hand-held antenna and a belt receiver so you can try to track him if he gets close to your location. I'll send them up on the Trailways bus but you won't get them until tomorrow. And I've got Bert Smith coming down from Altona with his gear. Maybe you can team up with him."

Wash was looking at the large map pinned on the wall behind the radio. He found the tree farm, traced the direction of the power lines marching past Methodist Hill and toward an area known locally as Cold Brook. A chill shivered up his spine.

"Dale," Wash said in a thick voice, "look at your map. Number Two could be headed for Cold Brook."

There was a pause. "Yeah. That's a big deer yard about eight miles west of you, isn't it, Wash?"

"That's right."

Another pause. "Then we got a problem, Wash. Remember what happened to Number Four."

"I remember. Brainworm."

Moose Number Four had been a magnificent animal. He had lived his solitary life in the foothills west of Raquette Lake when he had suddenly died. The students from the college had found him. The autopsy had revealed his death was caused by a parasite. Brainworm.

It was carried by deer and although it was harmless to its host the parasite was deadly to moose. It was transmitted by deer feces, the eggs passed through slugs and snails on the ground and deposited on leaves and brush which the huge animals would ingest.

The parasite could be concentrated in any area where deer stayed for a long period of time—like a deer yard, where they congregated to wait out the winter months.

"Maybe he'll turn north," Dale said, "before he gets to Cold Brook."

"Maybe," said Wash. "Maybe not."

"Right. If he does get into that area and beds down there we'll have to get him out. We sure as hell don't want to lose him."

"Yes, Dale, but that could take days."

Dale's voice was discouraged. "Right, it could. We would have to come in and put him to sleep and truck him out of there. We'd have to take some trees down to get a truck in and the local landowners would raise hell and probably get an injunction to stop us and Lord knows what all."

Both men knew that by then it would be too late; the animals would surely have become infected. Dale's voice became brisk again. "OK, Wash, he's not there yet and maybe he'll turn off in another direction. Team up with Bert tomorrow and keep me posted. We'll think of something."

"Right."

"Listen, we picked up something on the CB this morning. A man over near Chazy said he saw something last night, something as big as a horse. It might have been Number Two, Pass the word that if anybody sees him to leave him alone. All we need is a bunch of trigger-happy big game hunters."

"Sure." But Wash knew he wouldn't pass the word; it might get back to Buster Farvro and his cronies.

"OK, Wash," said Dale. "You'll get that gear tomorrow. I'll talk to you then. Over."

"Over."

Tomorrow might be too late. Number Two was traveling fast and he was headed in the Cold Brook direction and there were hours of daylight left.

Wash turned off the radio and stood in the middle of the room. Maybe Number Two would follow the swatch of the power lines where it angled north, away from Cold Brook. But there wasn't much forage along the lines, and Number Two was always hungry. Cold Brook was mostly cedar but birch and willow grew there and moose liked birch and willow.

Wash went to the closet and dug out his old service automatic. It was supposed to have been turned in when he was discharged but like thousands of other men he had kept it. With trembling fingers he shoved the recoil spring in place under the barrel and locked it. There was one loaded clip.

If Number Two wandered into the deer yard and if Wash was there to see him maybe he could scare him off. That is, if an animal that weighed three quarters of a ton and had no natural enemies could be frightened by an old man with a pistol.

Wash couldn't find the holster; he shoved the gun in his belt. As he started to the door he brushed against the stack of campaign posters and they fell off the table. That reminded him to turn back and leave a note for Nora. But she wouldn't be home, she was supposed to meet him at the town hall. He would try to leave a message for her there.

When Doc, the old collie, saw Wash put on his hat he whined and asked to go for a ride "No, Doc," Wash said and closed the door behind him.

In the spring and for most of the summer the deer yard was a swampy area fed by springs and a small stream. Under the trees the cover was thick with cedar bushes that crowded each other for sunlight and growing room. A hill shielded the area from the worst of the winter winds.

The deer were still on the higher slopes now, but with winter coming they would begin moving and many of them would return to this spot for shelter and to feed on the cedars. The ground had been trampled almost smooth and was heavy with deer droppings.

Wash locked the front wheel hubs on his jeep and shifted into four-wheel drive for the old trail ahead. Wash and some 4-H Club members used it to bring hay in to the deer if February was very severe and they thought the food supply might be depleted.

When the trail ended he had walked the rest of the way. He was tired, but he wanted to be on the west side of Cold Brook, facing the direction of the power lines that marched past the hill beyond the deer yard.

He slumped against a tree trunk and rested. The sky was as blue as he had ever seen. A brown squirrel ran impudently up to his feet and fled chattering through the trees.

He's miles away, thought Wash, maybe he's already turned off. He reached out and pulled a leaf from a bush and held it up to the sunlight. He saw the faint glistening silver tracks left by a snail. There could be the eggs of a brainworm on this leaf, the microscopic enemy that could bring down one of nature's most splendid creatures.

The squirrel chattered briefly from a branch above him. "When my great-granddaddy was alive," Wash said to the squirrel, "there were moose and elk and wolves all through these mountains. Wish I could have seen them like he did." He looked away and through a break in the trees he saw the peak of Whiteface. "Maybe your great-granddaddy saw them, too, little fellow."

The squirrel looked down with bright, curious eyes and sat motionless on the branch.

The shadows were growing long when Nora arrived at the town hall from the hospital. The parking lot was full and children milled about on the sidewalk. Evelyn Collins from the bank met her on the steps.

"Nora, Wash says maybe he can't come to the meeting."

"But I was supposed to meet him here."

Evelyn shook her head. "He called me this afternoon. Said he had to go see about something out at Cold Brook and to tell you he might be pretty late. Said it was about Number Two, whatever that is."

"That man!" said Nora.

"Not like Wash to miss an important meeting like this." It was Barney Freeman, dressed in a jacket and a string tie. Behind his heavy gold glasses his eyes were serious. "I do anything for you, Nora?"

"Thanks, Barney," Nora shook her head. She was worried and Barney could see it. "Wash is out there in the swamps somewhere and he ought to be here by now."

"Let's go fetch him then," said Barney.

"No, you go in to the meeting. I'll just drive on out there."

Barney pressed his lips together and shook his head. "No, ma'am. Wouldn't be right for me to have my say without Wash being there to argue with me. I'm coming with you."

Nora put her hand on his arm. "Thank you, Barney. I am afraid something might have happened to him."

"Better not have. I ain't done politickin' with him yet. The meeting can wait. My car's right over there."

"No, wait, Barney," Nora said. Her voice broke. "I've been out there. We'll need a truck or a four-wheel. I see Tom Carlton over there, maybe we can use his truck."

The worst of the pain had come and gone. He couldn't move his left arm or his leg or turn his head. The sun had been in his eyes for a while but now his face was in shadow. Wash lay where he had fallen under a big white pine and he watched the sunlight climb higher and higher on the trunks of the trees.

He heard the voices calling him but he could speak in no more than a whisper when he tried to answer. He was smiling when Nora knelt beside him and took his hand. Tears coursed down her thin cheeks.

"Wash, honey." Her voice was faint and she was crying softly.

Wash's eyes were shining. "I saw him, Nora," he whispered. "I saw Number Two. He was beautiful, Nora."

"Don't try to talk, Wash." Barney handed her his jacket and Nora spread it over her husband.

His voice was faint and slurred. "Tell Dale...tell Dale he's headed north...away from here...I watched him..."

Wash closed his eyes. It was silent in the woods and the last of the sunlight was high in the tops of the trees. A blue jay flew down and flickered past.

Barney put his hand on Nora's shoulder. "I'll go get some help," he whispered. "A stroke?"

Nora nodded. "I've seen it in the hospital. Tell them to bring oxygen."

"You want to try to move him, Nora?"

She looked around at the trees and the hill and the blue flash of another jay. The ground was cold and Wash had been lying there for a long time. She read the signs of damage, the pallor, the chill, the slackness.

"No," she said finally. "Let's not disturb him. If he's going, this is a good place as any."

Wash opened his eyes and looked at Nora. "Did I tell you, Nora. I saw him and he was beautiful..."

"Yes, Wash. All your animals are beautiful."

Wash looked up at the sky and tried to smile. "And you... Nora..."

He closed his eyes and she felt his hand tremble and then it was still.

Number Two didn't bed down that night. He was a bit hungry and the moon was full. No insects annoyed his ears or buzzed around his enormous drooping snout. He walked along a road that had a hard surface, which made his progress easy.

A red fox appeared at the side of the road, gazed at this big creature for a moment, and silently disappeared. An owl marked his passing with a plaintive hoot. The night was peaceful and still, with only small sounds from tiny things in the underbrush, and the slow thud of the creature's hooves.

There would be other moose in the Adirondacks soon, cows as well as bulls, and there would be pairings and offspring. But tonight Number Two was heading north, back to the hospitable prairies of Canada.

About the Author

Bill Lowe lives and writes in the Adirondacks in Ausable Forks, N.Y, close to the Ausable River and less than 15 miles from Lake Champlain. An Army Air Corps Captain in World War II, he later worked for a variety of advertising agencies, eventually settling in the North Country where he and his wife built and for 17 years operated the highly successful Hungry Trout Restaurant.